THE KILLING LABEL

By Ryan Alcock

Pale corpse by Moonlight

Twisted beauty hides behind

The killing label

Anonymous

Dedicated to Bronte

A catalogue record for this book is available from the National Library of Australia

THE KILLING LABEL

I

Bella North-Spectra was whining and it was, quite frankly, irritating Dana Spectra beyond belief. The younger girl was on one of her current pet peeves, that being Dana should really be doing better in her career. In truth, Dana had a relatively good life as a model, even despite the fact that winning the Miss Green Earth competition had not propelled her to the international stardom and success that her younger sister thought it should.

"If you spent a little less time fighting gun smugglers and helping thieves escape global crime syndicates, you'd be more popular. Your followers are still in the hundreds of thousands, which is totally ridiculous for someone who was Miss Green Earth. And involved in the scandalous death of a billionaire. More people should be taking notice of this," Bella pouted.

"I could get an OnlyFans page," Dana suggested, playfully.

"That's not going to increase your followers, is it?" she growled, and Dana was a little disappointed her sister wasn't more stirred by the lascivious suggestion.

"I'd sign up for it," Jeremy, Dana's best friend and confidante, grinned.

"Thank you," Dana said, as Bella rolled her eyes.

There are copious time travel stories in science-fiction that endlessly preach the idea that ripples spread out from even the slightest event, such that a simple and subtle action in someone's life can have consequences that are much further reaching that would initially appear. Coming from a therapy session with her sister, Dana Spectra had had time to pause and look back to see the sheer enormity of how her life had changed with all the impact of a sledgehammer through a plate-glass window, thanks to meeting one person in a casino in Singapore. She was about to discover that something even simpler could have a more dramatic impact.

As they walked along Petrie Terrace, chatting to themselves, Dana blinked as she spied a black cat deciding to cross the road, with an arrogance that only a cat can possess. It watched cars zoom back and forth along Petrie Terrace, its green eyes deep in thought, and then it decided that it could possibly make it across the road. As soon as Dana realised what it was about to do, her heart dropped and she ran forward, her brain hoping desperately that cars would stop as she decided to cross the road.

She was not wrong, and the cars did indeed pull up, drivers shouting angrily as they blasted their horns at the blonde girl in the black mini-dress. But Dana didn't care. Traffic had been brought to a standstill, but she was able to get to the black cat, picking it up carefully and taking it across to where it wanted to go. The cat actually purred, contented that it didn't need to use its legs anymore as a human had decided to do that job instead.

As she came back to her friends, the smile on her face, dropped a little when she saw her sister and friend standing beside the occupants of one of the cars that had stopped. Dressed in dark blue, and wearing heavy vests with a number of pockets, Dana didn't need to see the "police" on their uniforms to know that she was in trouble. Well, she sighed, it wouldn't be the first time this year she had been taken into police custody.

She had got a surprisingly polite, Irish cop named Rosney who explained to her as a parent might to a three-year-old child, why it was important not to just randomly cross the road. They were going to let her go, not least because a number of drivers who had been there had spoken out for her when they discovered what she had been doing.

"And please, take the cat with you," Rosney said, shaking his head.

Less than an hour later, Bella raced into her room, holding the cat.

"Have you seen the headlines?" she demanded, sticking out her phone. **MODEL RISKS LIFE TO RESCUE CAT**.

"Wow," Dana murmured, as she saw the number of articles.

"Also I think the cat might be deaf," Bella added, dropping him beside Dana.

Within another hour it became **AUSSIE MODEL RISKS LIFE FOR DEAF CAT**, and Dana scowled at her sister who shrugged innocently. Looking at her IG account, which her younger sister kept for her, Dana saw a number of candid pictures of her and the cat. Bella, however, was more excited about something else, and she scrolled to the top of the account. Dana's followers had finally crossed the million mark. Thirty minutes later it was over two million.

#catmodel began to trend, along with #catsavior and #Danaspussy, the latter of which Dana rolled her eyes at, much to Bella's confusion, until she picked up on it. By the end of the day Dana's followers had crossed the five million mark. Almost the precise moment it did, her phone buzzed, and Dana saw that it was her manager, Christa Adams, and she wondered how much trouble she was in.

"Brilliant!" Adams said, though there wasn't a lot of excitement in her voice.

"What…?" Dana started, but Adams wasn't to be interrupted.

"I don't know which of you made sure your bracelet was included in some of those shots, but whoever it was deserves a medal."

"My bracelet?"

"It's Digné!" Adams said, as though Dana struggled to understand English.

"It was a present. It's a bit chunky, but I have to wear it when I go out with Jeremy because he gave it to me."

"I don't care about that! Your name is trending in association with Digné, and their people have only just bloody contacted my people. Clicks, Spectra! They love the story, they love your look, and they want you to be the new face of Digné!" Dana dropped the phone as the news sunk in. A brand ambassador for a major jewellery company? Oh my…

"Yeah, but what does that mean?" Bella said, having picked up the phone, and Dana snatched it away from her.

Adams replied with her usual steely composure "You're going to be fucking rich if *she* doesn't balls this up."

And so, one Thursday morning Dana had woken up and joined her best friend and sister on a trip into the city, dressed casually and ready for sun later, and the following morning she had awoken to being an overnight sensation. All thanks to a cat (whom Bella had named Dine – Dana wasn't quite sure why, and wondered if she had misheard Digné, but decided to leave it).

However, there was one more ripple that was to have an effect the following day.

"Hey, you know who's followed you on IG?" Bella asked out of the blue.

"Honestly no," Dana replied. "A lot of creepy people, I'm guessing."

"Err, yeah, that's true," Bella admitted with a little grimace. "Though to be fair they followed you already. No, this is way more exciting."

"Do tell," Dana grinned indulgently.

"Millie!" The indulgent grin turned to a blank expression. "Bong-cha Nam!" Bella said. "Millie from G'Star!" That rang a louder bell, and Dana sat up from the couch.

"G'Star the pop group?" she clarified.

"Yeah, Millie is following you. Oh, so is Mee. You have two followers from G'Star! Oh my god, you should be following them back!"

Bella gushed.

"Well, fucking follow them back then!" her sister squealed, and Bella immediately began tapping away on the phone. "Wait, aren't there others?"

"Yeah, it's Millie, Mee, uh…" Bella paused, flustered, but Dana already had her phone out and was Googling.

"Bong-cha "Millie" Nam, Mee Bu, Soojin Sam and Aimi "Amy" Hirano," Dana supplied. "Follow them all. Oh my god, I can't believe famous people are following me!"

"I mean, Ophélie is not going to be happy," said Bella, raising an eyebrow pointedly.

"I mean more famous than me," Dana replied, a little annoyed. "Oh," she added, not looking up from her phone.

"Good oh, or bad oh?"

"Curious oh," her sister said. "Millie is the face of Digné in Korea."

"I mean," Bella began, a huge smile creeping across her face. "If that's not an excuse to go to a G'Star concert and meet and greet, what the actual is?"

II

Though she had a soft spot for Changi Airport in Singapore, Dana Spectra had to admit that Incheon Airport was mightily impressive. They had flown over it and Dana, sitting in a window seat, had the opportunity to see the airport from above, impressed at the symmetrical shape of the design, which looked to her a little like a claw hanging from a teardrop. Her flight having been booked by Digné (who had agreed with Christa Adams that Dana attending a G'Star concert would be brilliant promotion for the brand and create a lot of online chatter), Dana had to fly to Sydney to catch the Korean Air flight to Seoul. The consequence was reading an inflight magazine that outlined future changes to Incheon Airport which looked as though it was going to become considerably greener in the future.

Incheon was an airport that had won a number of awards over the previous years, and ranked in the top five airports for the past five years. More impressively it posted times of less than fifteen minutes for departure and arrival, and while it had followed the rest of the world with online booking and biometric check-ins, it was the AI robots named Airstar that were the revolutionary step forward. The short, squat, sleek white robots with touch-screens on their backs were multilingual and designed to assist passengers with a variety of services. Dana assumed that the plans to improve and update the airport would include more dependence on Airstar as time went on. As long as the system didn't crack under the pressure of the millions of passengers that went through the airport, it would be quite the revolution, Dana reflected.

She had spent most of the flight, however, catching on G'Star. It wasn't so much that she wasn't interested in the group; along with the likes of Blackpink and Twice, Dana very much enjoyed K-pop, but in truth G'Star was a new group she hadn't heard that much of. They were less the bubblegum pop of Twice and closer in style to the sexier, genre-bending Blackpink. Bella – who had more of an interest in K-Pop than she did – had told her that all K-pop groups have official colours, and their fans had their own names; G'star's colours were gold and white, their fans were called Glitter. Dana was a little sad she couldn't take her sister, but did promise her video messages and autographs.

"You are Glitter!" Bella intoned. "Don't forget it!"

Their music was catchy, but unexpected and some of the songs on their mini-albums (they had yet to release an album) were very different to what she thought the band would produce; moody, sensual stuff that defied the louder, in-your-face style of their A-sides. Songs like *Heol* and *Epic* had made the charts for obvious reasons, but it was *Wow* which captured her attention the most, and made her feel like she was in some strange, alien environment which unsettled her. A unique sensation, but one that made her fall in love with the group completely.

Millie, Mee, Soojin and Amy were also names she had forced herself to study. G'Star was not dissimilar to the mood of some K-Pop girl groups which utilised foreigners in their line-up. Aimi Hirano (or Amy) was Japanese and the youngest in the group. Bella had informed her that she was the *maknae*, literally the youngest who was generally regarded as the cutest, or perhaps sometimes the naughtiest. Certainly, from some of the online interviews it seemed that Amy had the cheekiest personality. She also seemed to share a close bond with Mee, a member who had been raised in London before moving back to Korea to join the group at the age of 14. Mee spoke the best English and was the "face of the group" when it came to interviews. Soojin, the oldest, was the main vocalist, and had a quieter, more background personality, though it was clear she cared about the other members deeply. That left Millie, the lead rapper of the group. The management team also deemed her the most beautiful of the group – she was the visual and centre. With her sharp features, surprising freckles and spiky short hair, she certainly caught the attention.

The Korean Air flight arrived at Terminal 2 of Incheon and Dana was forced to navigate through the long-carpeted corridors with the seemingly endless travelators in order to get to the actual Arrivals part of the airport. Here she was struck by how *white* the airport was. She wasn't certain whether that was just terminal 2 or if it applied to the entire structure, but with so much white – be it the speckled tiled floor, the reflective plastic around the shop fronts or light strips – she felt a little like she was on a spaceship in a science-fiction show. It didn't help that the entrances to the shops were rounded at the corners and designed to look as though they were on an angle. Add to that the random archways that were either mirrored or flashing multi-coloured lights, and Dana decided she was definitely on something that could be from *Star Trek*.

As she made her way through the terminal, she was surprised to see Airstar itself, moving along the corridor, chatting to itself in a variety of languages, including Japanese and English, and presumably Korean.

"Hello, my name is Airstar. Please come and say Airstar if you need any help from me." The robot was about the size of a teenager (probably Bella's height) and was essentially a white cylinder with a large screen on the front that flicked through a variety of different screens. On the top of the cylinder was a rounded head, also white, but with a black screen that had two big blue eyes picture on it. On its sides, two strips of lights cycled through a variety of colours, from purple to orange.

"Did you have a good time at Incheon Airport. Will you take pictures with me?" Airstar said, and Dana found it was now, inadvertently, directly in front of her. The screen showed two pictures, one of which indicated a photograph. Dana paused, and then lent forward and pressed the little Korean flag in the corner, which brought a menu that allowed her to change the text to English. She chose the photo option, and Airstar gave her the option of an email or SMS. Choosing the latter, the screen changed to a reflective image of herself, and Dana almost laughed out loud. She could see in the background other passengers looking curiously to see what she was doing. A large circle came up on screen, counting down from 3, and soon her picture was displayed, with *disagree* and *agree* options.

In truth, the picture wasn't that bad, so she agreed, and felt the vibration in her clutch as Airstar messaged her the photo.

"I love you dear. It is my gift. Please keep the memories. When you want to say goodbye to me, please press the goodbye button, or say Airstar." Dana looked around, catching the eyes of a wide-eyed little girl who smiled at her, entertained by the interaction. Dana lent forward and pressed the *goodbye* button that was now on the screen. "I'm returning home. See you later." With that, the robot rotated on its axis and then moved away from her. That was one for IG, she reflected.

It wasn't the most interestingly designed airport she had ever been in (it seemed that Changi had no competition here), but it was pleasant and reminded her in many ways of the Brisbane airport. She noticed that the white was broken up every so often by wood panelling and greenery and the roof in some areas had a curious triangle pattern that made up the skylights – though given that she had arrived in the evening it didn't look as impressive as it could. Nonetheless, looking out of the windows she could see the mighty city of Seoul throbbing away.

Dana had her various forms ready for submission and thanks to a mix of both these and the facial recognition the airport used, she was surprised to find that her arrival time had taken her roughly twenty minutes. After collecting her luggage from the baggage carousels, she exited into the greeting area on the first floor. There were surprisingly few people around, or to be more accurate, there were fewer people than Dana expected to be. She didn't feel crowded or forced into a flow of people. Instead, people quietly made their way to where they needed to be.

As in most airports, on passing through the Arrival exit, Dana saw groups of people standing around holding signs, which they waved excitedly as each new person exited in the hope that they would find the person they were looking for. Dana was slightly surprised to see some people standing around with cameras at the ready, and when they saw her and started snapping, she was even more surprised to find a large, burly Korean come up to her, bow and mumble her name.

"Err, yes?" she replied, not sure what to say, and the Korean man took her luggage and started to move, shielding Dana from the photographers. He shoved a card into her free hand and she looked at it, seeing her name printed neatly with the word Digné below it. Dana nodded absently, sliding the card into her clutch and following the man.

She tried to remember what her email from Christa had said regarding her trip into the city, but aside from *You'll be met at the airport by one of Digné's representatives*, it mostly escaped her. She could always check the email on the journey, she reflected, though briefly wished Bella was with her to keep her organised.

Once outside, the man released her and made his way towards a large, black Mercedes-Benz people mover. Dana was surprised to see that there were more photographers lurking around, and in the dark their flashes were far more obvious. However, it was when the man opened the door to the Merc that the flashes began in earnest.

He gestured to Dana to get in the car with some urgency, and she did, her mind logically reasoning that if that many people were taking photos of her getting into a car, it was unlikely that she was about to be kidnapped. Also, she was fairly certain that kidnappers didn't use Mercedes-Benzes. If they could afford that kind of car, they wouldn't need to ransom hostages.

Once inside, however, she realised that she wasn't really the target of the photographers. Seated in the car opposite her were two faces she immediately recognised, thanks to having spent an inordinate amount of time over the last few days looking at them. One was the oval-shaped, bright eyed face of Mee Bu, while beside her, looking as moody as always was Bong-Cha Nam, better known as Millie. Her sharp features were even more striking in real life and she could see the girl was wearing minimal makeup as her freckles were patently obvious. Both women bowed as she sat, but then Mee leapt forward and embraced her. Dana was a little astonished but happily hugged the other girl.

"I'm so happy to meet you," Mee gushed, her accent strangely English. "Millie and I were so impressed by everything you did for that poor little kitten. You're amazing!"

"I mean, it really wasn't that special," Dana said, spectacularly failing to comprehend quite what was going on.

"Can I hug you?" Millie suddenly asked, and Mee put her hand to her mouth.

"I'm sorry, I didn't think," she started, but Dana interrupted her.

"It's fine, honestly. Of course you can hug me. I can't believe you'd want to..." But this time it was Dana who was cut off as Millie leaned forward and pulled her close.

"When Digné made you the Australian face of their brand, I thought it would be the perfect opportunity to get to meet you," Millie said, though she never smiled and Dana found her impassiveness a little unsettling. She was very difficult to read, and Dana couldn't work out if the body contact was something to make her feel welcome, or a genuine emotion. Given what she knew of Koreans, the latter seemed unlikely.

"And then we were told you would like to see us in concert, and we couldn't have been more excited," Mee continued. Her hug had seemed more a product of her English upbringing which also explained her more Western sensibilities.

"Guys," Dana grinned, unable to reject Mee's infectious enthusiasm any longer, "you're one of the biggest groups in the world. I'm just an Aussie model who rescued a cat!"

"Not just that," Millie said, and she seemed to smirk a little.

"We met DJ Kabuki not so long ago."

"Oh, I wouldn't put too much stock in rumours," Dana waved her hand a little, though she tried to think back to what Kabuki could have told them. Certainly Karen Ichioka had been around when some of their friends had been murdered by a snake-eyed assassin, and she may have told her girlfriend some of that story. "We were in the wrong place at the wrong time," Dana added, hoping that she was right about what Kabuki had told Millie. The look on the Korean girl's face, however, didn't really suggest she believed it.

Dana was surprised at how easy it was to babble with the girls about mostly inane things, as they discussed Dine (the mere name of which sent Mee into gales of laughter, as she covered her face with both hands in a typical Korean gesture) and the sort of cat she was, as well as music that they liked in general. Despite appearing taciturn and rarely smiling, Millie had a cheeky sense of humour, but it was definitely Mee who had the most to say on the journey. Dana had noticed when she was watching videos of G'Star online that the girls' personalities appeared to be fairly close to what they presented – in interviews Mee and Amy tended to dominate the discussion, helped in no small part by Mee's fluency in English, while both Soojin and Millie would add in their own comment at various points. There was a playfulness to the foursome's public persona that was present in the real-life women in front of her. If they were putting on an act for her, it was a very good one.

Incheon was an island off the coast of South Korea, so to actually get to the city required travelling to get to the mainland. This brought Dana to mind of her relatively recent visit to Japan and travelling to Haneda Airport, though that certainly hadn't been as far away from the mainland as Incheon seemed to be which looked like it might take about an hour. As they crossed Yeongjong Bridge, Seoul opened up before them. At 7 pm at night, it looked like a piece of sci-fi anime, a futuristic city painted in gold and teal, with neon purples, pinks and oranges liberally splashed around. When Dana touched the window, a little in awe of what she saw, she felt the cold bite back at her and checked her phone to see that it was seven in the evening.

"How did you get time off from your rehearsals?" Dana suddenly realised, turning back to the singers in front of her.

"We've been at it all day," Mee grinned. "Trust me, when we arranged to meet you at the airport it was under strict instructions that we would be working our butts off during the day to make sure we are ready for tomorrow."

"Not that we don't work our butts off, right Nam Shik?" Millie turned to the front of the car where the large, burly Korean man who had first appeared at the airport turned and gave a wry smile. "He doesn't understand English," Millie continued, and Mee giggled.

"He probably thinks you're being mean," Mee said. She turned as well and spoke quickly in Korean to Nam, who furrowed his heavy brow and looked at Millie, though the older girl leaned over and slapped Mee on the arm.

"*Eonnie!*" Mee exclaimed, and got another slap.

"She just told him that I said he needed to lose weight," Millie growled and Dana bit her lip to stop the smile. Mee was still laughing at her own joke.

The rest of the journey passed in much the same way, and all three took selfies which they posted on their social media; Dana noticing that the simple #glitter was enough to get the attention of hundreds of thousands. When she saw that both Millie and Mee were tagging her, Dana suddenly realised the unexpected depth of her new found popularity.

"Where are we going?" Dana suddenly asked, realising she had no idea what her night was going to hold. Millie shifted across to sit beside her, though kept a respectful distance, and pointed out the window to the neon dream the Mercedes was travelling through, to a tall juggernaut of glass and metal that reached up to the sky, leaving the rest of the city far behind.

"Lotte World Tower," Mee supplied. "You're staying at the Signiel Seoul, one of the best hotels in Seoul. Did you not get told?"

"Oh wow," Dana murmured, the height of the building overwhelming her momentarily. She wondered if she should pretend she'd been kept in the dark, but couldn't bring herself to do it. "I forgot," she admitted, shamefacedly.

"It's the tallest building in Seoul," Millie whispered. "Fifth tallest in the world. At the top you can walk from the one side to the other via a skybridge. You have to do it."

"It'll terrify you!" Mee gushed. "Well, it terrified me. We did it for a promotional exercise."

"You don't live here, do you?" Dana said, turning to Millie, surprised to see the woman had moved closer.

"No, but the press think we do," Mee said, and she moved back to her original seat. "We have been here before with guests and we have a little system because there are always press waiting out the front when we arrive. So we go in, then we slip out the back way and the press never see us leave. So, they think we live there. The hotel is around the hundredth floor…"

"I think it's the thirty floors leading up to the 100th," Millie interrupted.

"And below that are apartments people can stay in," Mee continued, unperturbed by the interjection. "I guess that's where they think we live."

Dana nodded, her mind recalling Bella mentioning that the group all lived together, possibly in Lotte World Tower. Online, the "netizens" had argued it wasn't true, but one commenter had talked about how they often enter but never leave, which meant the set up was clearly working. She wondered if it was the girls' idea or someone else's. Perhaps the brooding Nam Shik, or was he simply security?

When the car had reached Olympic Road, an eight-lane highway that clung to the Han River, they had turned onto it and settled into the flow of traffic that eased along surprisingly quickly, all things considered. By the time that Millie had been able to point out Lotte World Tower, the Mercedes turned right into Songpa Road and continued forward, their destination now patently obvious.

Sitting in front of the tower was Lotte World Mall, a shopping centre which Mee described as amazing and promised they would go shopping at some point, though the obviously pragmatic Millie had warned her not to make promises she couldn't keep.

"We can barely go shopping anywhere these days," Millie explained, a little ruefully. "Do you get that?"

"Oh, no, not really," Dana said. "I mean, there are a few people who recognise me, but I don't get people crowding to get my autograph."

"I thought people might recognise you easier because of your favourite outfit," said Mee. "The little black dress with the white collar," she added.

"Oh," Dana exclaimed, a little surprised. "Yeah, I do like that style. And that dress in particular is a bit of a fave. I have a few," she admitted.

"I like it," added Millie, and she gave Dana a rare smile.

Two more lefts brought them firstly onto Jamsil Road, and then out the front of the Lotte World Tower itself. As the car pulled up, Nam Shik was the first to action, bounding out of the car and opening the door nearest the building, whereupon Millie and Mee got out, Millie grabbing Dana's hand on the way to help her down. The girls had been correct, and there were a number of photographers standing around, though unlike some paparazzi in other countries, these stayed a polite distance away, but began snapping regardless. Millie didn't let go of Dana's hand as the trio made their way through the glass doors into the lobby of the Tower, but even as they did, Dana noticed that Nam Shik wasn't their only company. Now they were joined by two more men in dark suits and turtlenecks, as well as a woman in an equally dark suit, but with a white collared shirt and round glasses, staring intently at her phone. A young man, in a less interesting grey suit, walked beside her, as obsessed with his tablet as his boss was with her phone. He kept whispering urgently to the woman, who nodded, but didn't seem able to reply.

By the time they were inside, Mee had linked her arm with Dana's, and Millie continued to lead the way, her hand never letting go of Dana's. The entourage that had formed around them had only increased the attention of the photographers outside, who continued to snap in an attempt to get something of interest from inside the lobby of Lotte World Tower.

Dana barely got a chance to take in the lobby, and had only glimpses of a curved ceiling and walls of glass as she was bustled towards an elevator. By now they had picked up a few more members for their entourage, one of whom was dressed in a neat, deep purple suit with a crisp white shirt that was buttoned to the collar, but had no tie. His grey hair was carefully styled, matching the equally grey mustache and pointed beard, while the bright white frames of his glasses ensured his face was the thing that grabbed the attention.

"Dana?" he purred with a smooth French accent, "how do you do? I am Mainard Descoteaux, I am the public relations vice-president of Digné, such a pleasure to meet you." He was able to talk and shake hands without breaking the stride of the team that they were with, as well as successfully not getting in between any of the girls to do it. "Millie, a pleasure as always," he added, and Dana noticed he gave a small nod to the woman with the phone, as though they too had already met. As he continued, the group all entered the elevator, which was a convenient size, given the amount of people who had gotten in. A woman in a long, deep blue dress, who seemed to be Descoteaux's assistant, pressed a button, clearly setting the destination for the group.

"Can I say how excited we all are at Digné with what is going to happen tomorrow night. A G'Star concert is, of course, one of the most exciting things that can happen, but to know that our two most recent ambassadors will be there, unveiling one of them, all of which is a massive thrill for everyone. The timing could not have been better, and the fact your Ms Adams came up with the suggestion is a master stroke. We couldn't have planned this better if we tried."

"I'm really excited to be here," she said, suddenly feeling that she could have come out with something better.

"Of course, we have sorted out everything that will be needed for your attendance tomorrow. Ms François and I have been working on your accessories, and I think I have something you will fall in love with."

"I have a few things prepared, and you are welcome to pick anything that suits you," the lady in the blue dress said, turning to Dana, a tablet in her hand. "Hair and makeup are ready to go. We have Sasha Song booked in for tomorrow at 4 to get your make up done, and we'll be here around 2 in order to have your outfit ready to go."

"*Parfait, non?*" Descoteaux gushed.

"The girls have to be ready for tomorrow. We can't keep them out much later," the woman in dark suit suddenly announced, and her grey offsider whispered something to her in Korean. "Millie, Mee," she said simply, and the girls looked a little flustered.

"We can settle her in, can't we?" Mee said. "She's new and doesn't know anyone. We can't just abandon her." The man in grey whispered again to the woman in the dark suit, who frowned and seemed unimpressed.

"We go up, we go in, we settle everyone, and that's it. We're gone. The concert isn't going to start late because of Digné," the dark suit woman said, and a flash of annoyance crossed Descoteaux's face.

"I wouldn't expect that of course, but given the money that is being donated to the concert, a little consideration of the night before would be appreciated," he said with an obvious dash of tension, and the dark suit woman made a face, before speaking.

"Of course," but the concession couldn't have been more reluctant.

The elevator reached the 92nd floor of Lotte World Tower and the group stepped out, with Ms François leading the way.

"Have I been checked in?" Dana wondered to herself, but she felt Millie squeeze her hand.

"Everything's been taken care of, I guess," the Korean girl assured her, but Dana had to admit she was feeling more flustered than she had been in quite some time. For a moment she wished that the two pop stars had the ability to stay with her, as despite being in a crowd of what now seemed to be more than ten people, Dana couldn't feel more alone. The reassuring physical contact of the G'Star girls was going to disappear and Dana wasn't even sure who she'd be left with.

As they continued down the corridor, Descoteaux seemed to be having an intense conversation with the woman in the dark suit, and both whispered urgently to each other, clearly feeling that their needs weren't being met.

They paused at 9204, and Ms François swiped a card on the door, opening it and standing back to allow everyone entry. Mee entered first, taking Dana and Millie with her. Exactly who followed in what order was lost on the model as she gazed around the room she had entered. The room felt like a traditional Korean room, even down to the padded cushions on the floor around the small wooden table with the simple, white porcelain crockery on it. It was separated from another room by doors that seemed to emulate *shoji* screens and could be used to shut the adjoining room off. This made sense as it was a bedroom, complete with a large, double bed on one side and a television set up on a row of wooden cupboards on the other.

Floor to ceiling windows gave a stunning view of the Han River and the brightly lit night side of Seoul shone through, though again this vista could be shut out with the upgraded *shoji* screens. Large water colours hung on either side of the bed, and in the other room as well behind the table, and small vases with delightfully non-Australian plants were scattered around on the various wood cupboards.

"The Korean suite," Ms François said as she handed Dana the door card.

"It's so beautiful," Mee gushed. "The bed is amazing. Can I try it out?" Dana paused, unsure of what to say to the request and not quite sure what was meant, but Millie shot a meaningful look at the others in the room and Mee's enthusiasm waned. Dana sighed a little as she realised that this was a work visit and they would have to start listening to what was being said.

The woman in the dark suit said something to Descoteaux in what was presumably Korean, but Dana couldn't pretend to understand it, though both Mee and Millie quickly snapped to attention.

"We have to go," Mee muttered, though again Dana wasn't entirely clear on why she was whispering, feeling as though her visit was going to leave her perpetually confused. "Our manager wants us to be ready for tomorrow's concert and we have a lot of work to do. I can't wait to see you then and introduce you to the other members." She bowed a little and Dana quickly stood up and bowed back, not entirely certain it was the right thing to do, but it seemed to spark a small wave of bowing from the manager and her assistant as well. Millie bowed a little and also gave a little wave, but by then the manager was ushering them out of the suite. At the door Mee turned and brought her thumb and forefinger together in a heart gesture. The door closed, leaving Dana and the Digné company alone.

"You probably want to have some rest," Descoteaux said, smiling, and Dana noticed that the smile rarely reached his eyes. "We'll have everything ready for you to start at two tomorrow, if that suits. Ms François has sorted out your make-up, hair and accessories. I have a collection of things right here," and he handed across his tablet to her, "that you can sort through and choose for what to wear. We're assuming you're going to go casual for the concert." Dana nodded absently as she flicked photos across the tablet, recognising cut out jeans from the likes of Dolce & Gabbana and Roberto Cavalli. She was of a vague mind to wear something a little daring, but was also conscious of what the standards were in Korea. Despite ostensibly being edgy, in truth the country preferred a little more modesty, and that applied even more with their music idols. Attending a concert baring too much would make things awkward for Millie and Digné, and Dana wasn't prepared to do that to the people who were being so kind to her.

Especially not if it was going to make her some solid money.

"I've got the important accessories sorted," grinned Descoteaux, and this time it did reach his eyes. "You and Millie will be a small fortune each, but the publicity of the two of you together will be completely worth it for us, particularly ahead of both of you recording some advertisements." He pronounced the word to emphasize the 'tise'. Dana smiled, suddenly feeling a little overwhelmed and she handed the tablet back to Descoteaux who shook his head.

"No, no, choose what you want and then get it to us in the morning if you can, and we'll make sure they are ready for you to wear tomorrow afternoon."

"Right, yeah," Dana nodded.

"You are overwhelmed," Descoteaux nodded, and dramatically began to usher his people towards the suite door. "Out, out the poor girl needs some rest!"

Ms François was the first to the door and she opened it, but to everyone's surprise there was a member of the hotel staff standing there, dressed in his uniform dark suit. There was a pause as everyone felt the awkwardness, but the staff member bowed and then handed over what he had been carrying to Ms François.

It was a bunch of white flowers and he said something which Dana only partly caught – *him-nay shay-o*. She had no idea what it meant, or even if she had heard it correctly, but curiously everyone in the room seemed as puzzled as she was, with the exception of one Descoteaux's staff who was Korean. He looked…haunted, almost. Descoteaux laughed a little.

"It looks like you can't escape the gifts," he said, though it seemed a little forced. "Come, come, let's leave Ms Spectra to her night." He bustled everyone through the door, but the last one to exit was the Korean gentleman and he turned to Dana.

"Be careful," he said quietly.

"Err, OK," replied Dana, by now very puzzled.

"The flowers," he added and then walked out. Dana frowned as the door closed and wandered over to the flowers. She took a picture of them and put them into a picture search where it returned nothing particularly interesting except that they were chrysanthemums.

Idly, she did a google search to see if there was any significance of chrysanthemums in Korea, and her immediate result was *a symbol of happiness and pleasure.*

Weird, Dana mused.

And then realised that the full sentence noted the flowers were originally from Korea, and that was what they meant to the Japanese.

She scrolled a little further down, when something caught her eye.

White chrysanthemums symbolise grief.

Usually given at funerals.

Be careful.

Dana got a slight twinge and she looked to her hand luggage which had been deposited on a chair. Inside was the soft case that had been given by Karim Narogin, the man from ASIO, which would hide her golden G48 Glock from airport security. She had been hesitant to bring it and to her own annoyance, her brain chose being very careful – be prepared for anything. The idea that she couldn't go anywhere without stumbling into drama was ridiculous really, but given that she had two recent incidents in her life which had brought her into contact with the spy fraternities of a half a dozen different countries, she was starting to feel a little paranoid. Her therapist had assured her that was to be expected and she needed to work on the idea that they might have been simply isolated incidents and would be unlikely to happen again. But when she had point blank asked her father if ASIO had a continued interest in her, he had looked guilty before assuring her it was unlikely. All of which led to the golden Glock being packed into her hand luggage and kept safely by her side should she need it.

Be careful.

III

The following morning Dana had set her alarm to ensure she woke early.

There was one particular touristy thing she was keen to do before she got ready for the big concert that night, and she wanted to make sure she had enough time for it.

On waking she had picked out what she wanted to wear for the night and emailed her choice through to the address that had been left on the tablet. Ms François appeared to be the hyper efficient type, and she replied in less than a minute to assure Dana that everything would be taken care of.

With that out of the way, Dana made sure to take a quick selfie with her back to the window, taking in the spectacular view of Seoul and the Han River that her room afforded her. It was amazing, and even though the morning had robbed the city of its neon glow, there was a beautiful golden wash over the buildings from the sun that brought everything to life. Seoul was quite spectacular and Dana wondered if she would have much time to explore it after the concert, given the advertising schedule planned.

She sent a few text messages to her sister and family, and made sure her social media was updated with the selfie, before heading out of the room to get some breakfast. Though there were a few nice restaurants in the hotel, her attention had been caught by the pastry salon on the 79th floor, but unfortunately it didn't open until 11. As such she opted for Stay on the 81st floor.

To her surprise she was welcomed on arrival, and ushered inside as a special guest. Although this seemed puzzling, her phone had begun to buzz, and when Dana risked a glance, she saw that her sister had started sending her messages about the news reports on her arrival and meeting with the girls from G'Star. This, it seemed, was quite big news. There were also rumours about what she and Millie would be wearing, with some eerily accurate. Dana shook her head, but at least understood the sudden interest in her, and she pocketed her phone.

As she did, though, something – or more accurately someone – caught her eye. She swung around to get a better view, but what she had thought she saw was no longer there. There was no sign of the curly, black hair and the off-the-shelf suit she thought she had seen.

"Spectra-*ssi*?" the waiter that was attending her said, and Dana turned and bowed her head, muttering sorry. He guided her over to a small table with a bright yellow chair, at which she sat down and gratefully took the menu. For the first time she inhaled the various aromas that were wafting around the room, the smell of fresh fruit and coffee, blending with the hot, sweet pastry and egg. It was sumptuous, and she could feel her mouth-watering, so she quickly summoned her waiter back and ordered (her natural instinct had been to wait, but she had heard that in Korea it was not considered impolite to summon the waiter).

Dana finished her meal of fresh fruit, croissants and sweet Earl Grey tea, and after a brief conversation with the waiter about payment (which, he assured her, would be attached to her suite so was not something to be concerned about), she set off for the elevator once again. This time her destination would be much further up than her personal floor.

She had dressed in a set of V9 performance tights, along with an athletic singlet, both in black and both from Bodyscience. They had been sent complimentary to her at some point in the past week, and she felt she should probably try to get some pics of them on her social media. When Mee had told her what Lotte World Tower was noted for, she knew precisely the best pics to get.

Lotte World Tower stands at 123 floors, the top of the building peaking at almost 555 metres. It is one of the five tallest buildings in the world, and the hotel section occupies floors 76 to 101. Floors 42 to 71 are residences, while 14 to 38 is office space. 105 to 114 are more office space, but floors 117 to 123 are occupied by Seoul Sky, a set of observation decks which is nothing short of astonishing. And Seoul Sky gives access to the Skybridge – a relatively thin bridge open to tourists, linking the top two peaks of the building.

In truth, Dana had first made her way to the lobby to find out what was the best way to get to Seoul Sky as it was clearly not possible to simply jump on a lift at some point and get there. Most lifts started from the very bottom of the building so that the general public had as much access to the decks as anyone else. The clerk had politely (and profusely) apologised that unfortunately there was indeed no easy way to get to Seoul Sky from the hotel. What Dana hadn't noticed the night before on her hurried and flustered arrival was that the building has been designed to have different access points for different facilities. Nonetheless, the clerk did say that she was able to book Dana access to Seoul Sky and also the Skybridge, which she was more than happy to do.

On a whim Dana asked for two tickets to the Skybridge. She had vaguely hoped she might get someone to accompany her, but that now seemed unlikely.

It turned out that aside from having to take a 79-floor journey down to the lobby only to take a 117-floor journey back up again, things were relatively straightforward. The queues were surprisingly short, all things considered, and the journey up was much faster than the journey down, helped in no small part by the elevator being a series of screens which, as it went up, displayed a video which suggested the elevator was moving horizontally. It was a strangely unsettling experience, but those around her let out appreciative oohs and aahs, and Dana felt a little like the Grinch for not being more impressed.

However, as she stepped out of the elevator and was ushered forth, she saw what she thought she had seen earlier – the off-the-shelf suit and the black curly hair. There were a number of people standing around in dark blue uniforms, clearly security or at the very least guides, and Dana marked them all out before making her way from the alcove that housed the elevators out and across to the observation deck.

This deck stood out from the building and had a glass floor which allowed people to not only look out of the windows at the spectacular view of Seoul in the morning, but also the dizzying drop that was directly below them. Dana didn't have a particular fear of heights, but she had to admit that even she felt her stomach lurch when she looked down at the drop below her. She took a little gulp and looked up, noticing that a number of people were less-than-surreptitiously taking photos of her. She gave a little smile and a wave, and they bowed, which made her bow back. A person with short spiky white hair and eyes so dark they seemed black, took a quick photo, but there was no smile on the androgynous face. Dana gave another quick wave, feeling uncomfortably exposed.

This gave her, though, the opportunity to step away from the floor and head to the corridor that led to the other side of the building. On her left were windows allowing her to view the city still, but the right was a wood panelled wall. As she moved around there was a doorway into a disabled toilet and Dana quickly opened it and slipped inside. She kept the door ajar to peer out of. She had drawn enough attention to herself such that she hoped the person who was following her would take the bait.

Sure enough the suit walked passed the door. As the figure walked past, Dana pulled the door open and grabbed the man by the back of his jacket, yanking him into the toilet and closing the door with a foot, even as she shoved him up against the wall, twisting his right hand around and up his back.

Colonel Indigo Spectra had decided that since his daughter had recently had two run-ins with Interpol, it was for the best that she got a little self-defence training. This suited Dana perfectly, as she had decided on her return to Australia that she wanted to be a little more capable in a fight, rather than just attacking like a blunt force object. As such, Karim Narogin whimpered as his arm was pushed further up against his back.

"You're going to fucking break it, Spectra!" he whined.

"Why are you following me, Karim?" Dana hissed in his ear.

"I need to talk to you," the man replied. "Fuck's sake, seriously, Dana, let me go." Dana released him, and he turned to her. He was the same man she remembered, short and scruffy, with wild, black hair and deep brown eyes – a testament to his Indian and Indigenous ancestry.

"I don't work for ASIO," Dana said, and leant back against the sink that was on one side of the room. Karim looked around and then shrugged as he sat down on the toilet.

"You're now what we like to call an asset," he said, rubbing his right shoulder.

"Not for you lot," growled Dana. "Not for anyone."

"Spectra, it doesn't work that way," Karim sighed. "It is what it is. If you're an asset, you're an asset. You don't get to decide whether you are or not. You are now one. Which, yes, it seems we share with Interpol."

"You can't tell me what to do, and neither can they."

"Look, you can have your hissy fit later," Karim sighed. "Let's just get over it for the moment and talk about the reason I'm here."

"It will be to take photos for my Instagram," Dana said with a characteristic smirk.

"You do that a lot, you know, that smirk."

"It's my thing. People know me for it," replied Dana, rolling her eyes. "What do you *want*, Karim? ASIO's not even supposed to operate outside Australia, are they?"

"You know which label G'Star is signed to?" Karim asked, ignoring the question.

"Of course," Dana said, before realising that she actually had no idea. "Not one of the big ones," she added lamely.

"It's called Moonlight," Karim supplied. "It's not one of the top five, but it is up there. They've had a fair few acts do well recently. Also they are part of a big move to create supergroups in K-Pop. But not just from their own talent – talent across the companies."

"Ok, so?"

"They've also had five artists die in the last year," intoned Karim, like some grim reaper.

"That's," Dana paused, wondering what to say. "Unlucky."

"Very," agreed the analyst. "In fact, if one were being cynical… unreasonably unlucky."

"Oh my god, why would ASIO possibly be interested in the deaths of K-Pop idols?" Dana sighed, suddenly seeing her fantasy trip taking a turn for the worse.

"Well, obviously nothing," Karim replied pointedly. "Except…"

"Except?"

"Do you know much the K-Pop industry contributes to Korea's economy? It's billions, by the way. You don't have to answer."

"ASIO thinks that some musical groups not even signed up to one of the big five music companies is an attempt to destabilise the Korean economy?" Dana almost laughed with incredulity.

"Well, not all of those deaths were Moonlight talent. Two occurred when Moonlight created their supergroups, so some talent did come from *the big five*. But even then, ASIS wouldn't normally show an interest," he conceded.

"ASIS?" Dana said, incredulously.

"There have been rumours, initially from the CIA but then…

others…that an idol may not be what he…or she seems to be." Karim suddenly seemed very awkward, as though he needed to tell someone that their pet cat had just died. Dana frowned slightly as her mind began to put together what she had been told.

"You think a K-Pop idol is a spy?" and the idea seemed almost as incredulous as her previous guess.

"Not every idol is from Korea," Karim reasoned. "Thailand, China, Japan," he began to list, but then paused. "North Korea."

And then suddenly it clicked into place.

"Oh my god, you think one of G'Star is a spy!" she blurted out, and Karim jumped up nervously, gesturing for her to keep her voice down.

"I didn't say that," he said, *sotto voce*. "I'm saying that ASIS think that," and he had the decency to look shamefaced about it.

"You're not seriously asking me to investigate them?" replied Dana, trying to keep the shock out of her voice.

"ASIS asked if they could use our asset," Karim began, and Dana found herself so furious she tugged at the door and stormed out of the toilet. Karim followed, blushing a deep red when a few of the other tourists looked over at him; an elderly Korean woman looking particularly disapproving.

Dana made her way back to the main observation deck and went straight over to the escalator that led to the next floor, Karim in tow desperately trying to catch up.

"Dana," he hissed, as she strode straight on from the escalator to the stairway that led up another floor.

"Excuse me," a blue suited Korean man stepped forward to Dana as she entered the SkyCafe on floor 122, "is that man bothering you Miss Spectra?" Dana turned back to Karim, a little satisfied to see him struggling up the stairs, and glowered, but turned back, her face full of joy.

"Oh no, that's just my chauffeur. We're going to the Skybridge. Is this the floor…?"

"Ah, no, you have to go up again," the attendant smiled warmly. "Would you care for a complimentary tour, Miss Spectra?" he asked politely, and Dana immediately smiled before accepting the offer. "If you would care to step this way, Miss Spectra, and, your friend," the attendant continued.

"Thanks," Dana grinned, and the attendant led them to the only elevator on the floor. Dana took a quick look and saw that it was indeed separate to the one that ran from the basement to the 118th floor. This one seemed to go up to the 123rd, where the exclusive 123 Lounge was located (Dana had glanced at the prices online and realised that it was probably not going to be an option for her).

"Wait a minute," Karim spluttered. "What do you think you're doing?"

"*We* are going on the Skybridge," Dana smiled sweetly.

"But, don't you have to book a month in advance or something? You can't go in the morning?"

"The joy of being a celebrity, it seems," replied Dana, and

stepped forward into the elevator which had arrived. Their attendant followed, and Dana paused to look at Karim. "Come on," she ordered. With a grimace the analyst stepped forward.

They exited the elevator into a lobby which seemed to have a pine floor with a stylised sand pattern against the wall (though presumably it wasn't sand). Dana could see the 123 Lounge itself, and exclusive VIP restaurant that was currently closed. The attendant led them in the opposite direction and soon the pair found themselves in a less impressive room, with racks of red jumpsuits and black strapping hanging from the wall. Here there was a woman in her thirties, her eyes lined from smiling and her black hair pulled back into a pony tail. She was wearing one of the red jumpsuits.

"*Anyeong!*" she grinned at them. "My name is Dahyun," she bowed as she spoke to them, and both Dana and Karim returned the gesture, "and I'll be your guide for today on this very special trip. Lucky for you I was around," she added with a wink. "The jumpsuits are there if you want them, but you're not obliged to wear them. They provide a bit of protection from the wind, but you'll probably not feel the cold," she added almost laughing. "The good thing about them is that you can attach your phone so if you drop it, it won't fall 541 meters!"

"Can we leave our phones somewhere safe?" Dana asked.

"Of course," Dahyun replied. "I can take them and lock them up safely."

"Oh good, then you can use my phone to take pictures of me," Dana said to Karim, raising her eyebrows.

"Wait, I'm not going up there!"

"You absolutely are," replied Dana. "If you want me to give slightly more than no thought to what you were talking about earlier." She put her hands on her hips, watched by the bemused Hyun. Growling, Karim stormed over to the jumpsuits to find one that fit him. "I'll just wear this," Dana said.

"No problem," Dahyun replied, but it felt forced and Dana sensed she disapproved of the decision. "You'll still need to wear the harness though, that is an absolute must."

"Oh yeah, of course," agreed Dana, and she took the harness that Hyun handed across to her, stepping into it and bringing it up over her shoulders. Hyun got behind her and made some final adjustments, tightening it so that it closed around Dana's body. Karim got the same treatment, looking miserable in a jumpsuit that managed to look like it was oversized.

"Right," Dahyun said, "we're going to go up some stairs, and it's a bit of a journey. It's also a bit dark, so your eyes will take a moment to adjust when we get to the Skybridge. There are, however, a few more small points of safety I need to go through with you."

IV

It was about twenty minutes later when Dahyun pushed open the door that led to the platform that the Skybridge stretched away from, making its way to the opposite structure. Dana was mildly regretting not wearing the jumpsuit, as the wind whistled and blew her hair around, biting into her bare arms. Beside her Karim was almost pale.

"I can't believe you're making me do this," he whispered.

"Yeah, well, if you want something from me, you'd better be prepared to earn it," Dana growled back. "You need to take pictures of me as I'm crossing the bridge. Make sure I look great. Get the clothes, and try and get the background."

Dahyun was busy clipping the harness to the safety rope, and both Dana and Karim felt the strong tug as the guide tested to make sure that they were safely attached. With that, Dahyun turned to them.

"We're going to cross the bridge now," she said, the grin still on her face. "Make sure you place your feet carefully so that you don't step on nothing," she added. "I would say you shouldn't look down, but that sort of misses the point!" With that, the Korean woman strode confidently onto the bridge and began to cross. Dana gave Karim a side glance and a wink, and then walked over to the bridge. For the first time she could see how thin the bridge seemed to be, and how flimsy it was. Made of metal, it still looked like the sort of wooden bridge that connected trees in forests; not much wider than two meters and the bridge itself was made of metal slats. When Dana looked at her feet, she noticed that some of the slats were spaced further apart at the beginning of the bridge, meaning she would have to treat them like stepping stones. Cautiously she placed her foot on the first panel and then stepped onto the next one.

The height was dizzying and Dana lost all sense of the cold as her body activated its panic responses. She could feel herself starting to sweat. Strangely, she had made her way across a bridge quite high up a few months back in Switzerland, but at 541 meters above ground, Dana's imagination played overtime as she realised were she to slip through the slats and fall down the tower, she would be nothing more than a rag doll.

"Come on, there's nothing to worry about," Dahyun said and waved at her. Dana took a little gulp and took another cautious step across the next gap, her hands gripping the railing so hard her knuckles were white. She risked a glance behind and was a little surprised to see that Karim was indeed taking pictures, and with her image at risk she straightened her back and took a few more steps until she met up with Dahyun in the middle of the bridge.

By now Karim had put the phone away and grabbed the railings to walk across and join Dana and Dahyun. Dana was impressed at how the little man was coping, though she noticed that he still looked very pale as he reached them.

"What I want you to do now," Dahyun said to them, "is a couple of star jumps! *Hana dul set!*" With that she did a star jump, demonstrating what she wanted. "*Hana dul set!*" she called again, and this time Dana joined in, though she suspected her feet never left the ground. From the grin on Dahyun's face she knew she was right.

"*Hana dul set!*" and the three all jumped. Dana turned to Karim to congratulate him on what he had done, but several things happened at once which were a little bit distracting. The first was a strong gust of wind which pushed them to the side of the bridge, and all three grabbed the rail to support themselves, but Karim dropped the phone in the process which fell, though thanks to the jumpsuit, merely ended up around his knees. At the same time, Dana saw someone close the door on the platform they had come from.

Someone else had been on the platform?

"Is there anyone else up here?" Dana turned to Dahyun.

"No, just you. Special treatment for a star," Dahyun grinned. "Moonlight has a lot of pull. Why don't you sit down on the bridge and dangle your legs over the side?"

"You're not serious?" gulped Karim.

"Everyone does it," came the effusive reply. Dana couldn't help but smile, and she lowered herself carefully.

"I suppose you want photos," grumbled Karim, and he reached for the phone, but as he did, Dana realised that the bridge was more slippery than she had initially thought. Her left foot gave way and she felt Dahyun's hand under her arm.

"Careful," the guide said.

"Right," Dana replied, both hands gripping the rail. She frowned as a strange smell reached her nose, but as she lowered herself again her feet gave way one more time. There was something on the bridge that stopped Dana getting a grip, and she felt her feet slip out from under her and through the gap.

Her bum hit the bridge, her legs straight out in front of her, but she could feel the momentum moving her forward, and whatever it was that had made her feet slip also made her backside slip as well, and she could feel her whole body sliding forward. Desperately she grabbed at the metal rope but her body pulled her down and her hands stung as the rope pushed into them, forcing her to release her grip automatically.

Both Karim and Dahyun were shouting, but Dana couldn't understand them as the wind whipped up around her. Her body continued to fall, and she looked up, grateful for the safety rope, and realised that there had indeed been someone at that exit. The other end of her rope flew untethered along the bridge. Karim must have understood what was happening as he reached out to grab the rope, but only one hand was successful, so he was yanked forward, dragged to the gap that Dana had slid through.

Dahyun's experience kicked in quickly and she too grabbed at the rope, but it sheared through her hands. Dana's stomach lurched as she continued to fall, unable to do anything except watch her potential saviours. She saw Karim slide under the gap, but to her surprise he twisted his body around so when he slid off the bridge, he managed to fall on the other side of the bridge rail, resulting in him becoming a counter balance for Dana, whose fall jerked to a stop. To his credit, Karim had grabbed his side of the rope with both hands and was clinging onto it for her dear life.

Much lower than the little spy, Dana paused for a moment, not daring to make a movement in case the rope was somehow cut through by the metal siding. Cautiously she grabbed at it and tested to see if she could pull herself up a little. Karim refused to release his grip on the rope, and Hyun had reached down to start pulling Dana up to safety.

It took a surprisingly short time before Dana could grab hold of Dahyun's hands and between them Dana was hauled back onto the bridge. As soon as she had her knees on the bridge, Dana started pulling the other side of the rope, dragging Karim up, and with Dahyun's help the trio were back on the bridge again.

"We have to get you off," Dahyun said, grabbing hold of Dana's arm, and Karim did the same. Together they returned to the safety platform. Dahyun kept glancing around, and Dana wondered if the tour had been filmed. If it was, that was something she was definitely interested in looking at when she had a free moment.

V

Dana Spectra and Karim Narogin were seated in the 123 Lounge at 11.56 am, both sitting drinking water, though more elaborate and certainly more alcoholic drinks sat in front of them. Through the speakers the moody sounds of (G)I-dle were being piped, and the view from the window in front of them was undeniably spectacular.

However, if you had seen that view hanging from an untethered safety rope, the appeal tended to evaporate. The news was already reporting the incident, a news helicopter having captured some of the action and Christa Adams, along with Mainard Descoteaux had called to ensure that everything was alright. Police were talking with Dahyun, but Karim had managed to make them disappear allowing Dana to get a moment's rest, which she was genuinely appreciative of.

"I don't want to say I told you so," Karim began, finally breaking the silence between them.

"You shouldn't, because it doesn't make any sense," retorted

Dana.

"You can't say that was an accident," protested Karim.

"I'm not saying someone didn't try something, but how could they possibly know I was the target?"

"Wasn't it Moonlight representatives that set up the bridge walk? Maybe even a member of G'Star in particular?" Karim put his drink on the table and sat back, his arms crossed with a satisfied argument-winning look on his face.

"It's such a leap, Karim," Dana whined, petulantly. "Surely the Korean secret service…" She paused for a moment. "Wait, does South Korea have a secret service?"

"Err, I think it's pronounced *Daehanminguk Gukgahangbohwon Gukseongwon*," Karim replied. "It's the National Intelligence Service. When it was set up it was the Korean Central Intelligence Agency, of all things. It's one of those organisations that have had their powers restricted a fair bit since democracy was achieved. And, Eastern intelligence services tend to be very protective of their information when it comes to the West," Karim shrugged.

"Out of curiousity, how open is ASIS to the NIS?" Dana asked, sitting forward. Karim opened his mouth to argue, and then shut it again, clearly unwilling to outright lie.

"Yes, alright, they don't exactly play fair either," he grudgingly admitted. "The thing is, maybe the Koreans have looked into this K-Pop star, maybe they haven't, but you have to admit there's something very odd about the deaths."

"I still don't understand why it bothers ASIS so much. Or the CIA for that matter," Dana added. "Why not just get Interpol to work out a communication channel between you guys?"

"I never thought I'd hear you advocating for Interpol," Karim grumbled.

"Look, outside of its crappy operatives, I'm sure the whole idea of it is great," Dana said. Her water had finally run dry and so she grabbed the red drink in front of her.   "What is this again?"

"Negroni," Karim said. "Should give you back some of your energy."

Dana took a sip and pulled a face. "I hate gin," she said. "Just for future reference."

"Of course you do." Karim leaned forward. "Look, can you just keep an eye out or something. Do that thing you do to get into people's," he paused for a moment as Dana shot him a look that could have comfortably melted the glass window behind him. "Heads," he finished, and the relief was almost tangible. "It would be better for us to know if there's a North Korean spy, especially if the Koreans already know and just can't be bothered telling us."

"I don't even know how I'd do it," mumbled Dana, taking another sip and wincing. She looked around and noticed that the room was starting to fill up. There were a number of flashes from photographers and Dana wondered if the press had found her, but she realised that she wasn't the target as she overheard someone saying *Boom*. Bella's lessons had included the name Boom – a K-Pop idol of some repute and definitely more interesting than her. She had a little under two hours before her preparation began, and she had to admit she was feeling shattered. She closed her eyes and for a moment didn't want to open them again. The thought of drifting to sleep and not waking up was more enticing than anything else that was on offer at that moment. She let out a deep sigh, not sure if it was at the fact she couldn't sleep or Karim's request.

"Fine," she said, placing the glass back on the table. "I'll see what I can do. But for the record, I think you're wrong about this."

"Cool, prove me wrong," Karim replied, slumping down in his chair. "Oh, here's your phone," he added, realising it was in his jacket pocket. Dana took it and absently flipped through the photos. The ones of her posing on the bridge were quite impressive, she thought. The background was astonishing and the wind made her hair blow like she was a superhero descending from the skies. Plus her ass looked amazing in the leggings. That was definitely going up on the social media sites.

The next along, was a video of her walking across the bridge and doing star jumps. Well, sort of doing them. Her fear must have got the better of her, as she wasn't quite the monument to confident athleticism that she thought she had been, her arms never straying too far from the sides of the bridge.

Then there was another video. It was difficult to make out in many ways, as it started with Dana lowering herself to slide her legs off the bridge, but her fall was captured in all its glory before the picture went crazy, presumably as Karim let go of the phone. The entire incident was captured, though not particularly well; the camera flipping around taking in Dana dangling on the end of her rope, and Karim scrabbling to grab the other end. She pulled the video back a bit and looked again at her feet sliding. There was definitely something there, some sort of clear liquid. Not water…it was thicker than that.

"Did you smell something when we up there?" Dana asked of Karim. "Like," she paused trying to remember the smell.

"Fish?" Karim said.

"Yeah but…fish oil," Dana mused.

"You think someone put fish oil on the bridge?"

"No, but what sort of clear liquid smells like fish oil," wondered Dana.

"No fucking idea," replied Karim, and he grabbed his Negroni, swigging it back quickly. Dana shut down her phone and sat back in her chair. Across from her, the sun continued to rise above Seoul.

Someone really had tried to kill her.

VI

Having announced his need to leave, Karim Narogin took Dana's phone and plugged something into the port which immediately caused it to seemingly die. The little square device he had, however, immediately come to life and displayed a vast array of swift moving icons and moving bars. He turned the little device towards her and she saw her own face reflected, with the word *scanning* below it, and then asked her to press her little finger to the device. He then asked if she used her thumb or forefinger to activate her phone (she drily replied she used her face) and he nodded, asking her to touch her forefinger to the device, which was also duly scanned.

He handed the phone back to her with a small grin.

"Probably should have checked if you had the memory capacity for that, but fortunately you did. I figured you'd be a "only the best phone" kinda girl."

"What did you do to my phone?" Dana asked, glowering a little.

"There's a second phone beneath the first," Karim replied. "When you do your normal thing, you'll see that there's a small red dot in the top corner?" Dana frowned as she failed to see it, but then her eyebrows raised in surprise as the small little dot became evident. "Touch it with your little finger," Karim suggested, and Dana did as she was instructed. Her phone went blank, and then suddenly rebooted with a totally different set of apps. "Lots of little handy things there," Karim explained, "but the most important is that it's effectively a burner phone. If you used it to phone, it would read as a totally different number, and also sends the signal to at least two different towers, which means it can't be readily traced. Put in any numbers that you would only dial as an asset." Dana glowered again at the word, but didn't take the bait. "That way we can get you, you can get us, etc, etc."

"How do you get me if I've got my other phone on?" Dana asked.

"Oh, you'll feel a little vibration and the red light will blink. If you can't answer, we get voicemail. The other thing, if you press the red button with your forefinger…STOP!" Karim grabbed her hand as she was about to do it. "It will delete the background phone completely," Karim added.

"What, so it's easier to delete the phone than it is to use it?" said Dana patronisingly.

"Yes," replied Karim, his patience slightly gone. "So if someone forces you to, you can easily get rid of it in a simple move."

"Oh," Dana replied. "I suppose that makes sense."

"Another gift, courtesy of ASIO," Karim said acidly.

"Given they want me to spy on some girl they think might be a North Korean agent, it's the least they can do." Dana's reply was equally frosty.

"Well, true," conceded Karim.

"So why are you my handler?" Dana suddenly snapped indignantly.

"It turns out that no one was really lining up for the job," came the biting reply. "I was stuck with the job of dealing with you. I did point out I was an ASIO analyst not an ASIS spy, but apparently that wasn't enough to give me an excuse to avoid it."

"Thanks," Dana said, pulling a face. Karim raised an eyebrow.

"Good luck," he added, as he got up and left the restaurant.

Without paying.

Bastard.

Fortunately, when Dana left, she was told that the drinks were entirely complimentary after the incident. They were, naturally, she supposed, rather desperate for her not to sue them.

When she returned to her room, she realised that it was almost closing in on two, and for the first time that day she felt a slight weariness. After everything that had happened, she was ready for a rest, and yet the real action was only just beginning.

She turned on the TV to a shot of her dangling from the Skybridge, and wondered who had taken it, but it was unimportant. The article was clearly about her, and her picture featured prominently, alongside G'Star, which was probably not the publicity that anyone was hoping for.

For a moment she wondered what she should do, thinking to contact either her sister or Adams, but then she made the decision, and posted a set of photos to her social media accounts. For her story, she posted a small segment of the video of her sliding, captioning it: wasn't planning on hanging around, but sometimes you don't get to choose!

The moment she hit post, her account reacted, and there were so many messages that it was going to be impossible to read them all. She looked at the notification count increase, and then sent a text to Bella asking her to log in and do some responding. Bella replied quickly, asking if she was OK, but there was a knock at the door and Dana had little time to send anything other than a thumbs up.

When she opened the door, it was to a group of people, all of whom swept in and began setting up around the room. The dedicated Ms François led the pack, directing people to various positions and clearly indicating the correct order. Dana was sent to have a shower, and exited wearing nothing more than her white lace underwear, but no one in the room batted an eyelid, except for one gentleman who put a dressing gown over her shoulders before taking pictures with the phone he had brought.

For the next few hours, Dana was carefully brought to life. Sasha set to work on her face, while her hair was carefully coiffured into something that was absolutely astonishing. Dana had to admit that with the added extensions, her hair had been curled and styled such that it sat, almost in a seventies style, like a golden mane around her face. It was absolutely beautiful and something she would never have considered for herself, yet it looked amazing.

Her makeup, meanwhile, was just as incredible. With her clothing decision being a set of impressively ripped Roberto Cavalli jeans and a Calvin Klein lounge bodysuit, it was Ms François' choice of a blossom yellow cropped snow mantra parker by Angel Chen that added the colour and determined Sasha's make up direction. Dana's face was brought to life in shades of yellow, with her eyeshadow being a vibrant yellow carefully blended into a burnt orange, while her lipstick and blush was a bronze.

After four hours of work, during which Dana sneakily took photos and posted the various stages – as well as getting the all-important selfie with Sasha, who she was delighted to find she got along with particularly well – Dana was ready to go, and she had to admit she looked incredible. The outfit was chic, and modern and she looked, essentially, *cool*. Not some sort of fashion horse, nor something she'd got from her own wardrobe, but an image that her followers would love. Sexy and stylish. Dana's personal contribution was her Tresor Midnight Rose perfume. She had overruled the other choices and insisted on it, much to Ms François' disappointment.

However, it was the jewellery that the representatives of Digné were most keen to show off. There were five pieces in total, starting with an astonishing set of ear rings that contained a brilliant diamond in each. On her right ear was a cuff as well, which had been designed to look like a star falling towards the diamond earrings. The star was also a light catching diamond, with more diamonds in the stylised tail of the star. Around her neck was a necklace that looked like it was a set of golden rings attached together in a vaguely Grecian style. This was a slightly more colourful design as the front three rings were a ruby, a sapphire and an emerald with little diamonds surrounding them.

Ms François explained that the entire set was *universal* and the necklace represented a solar system with different planets orbited by their diamond moons. The exact same design, though slightly smaller, was matched on her wrist by the bracelet.

There was another bracelet, a much simpler golden chain, and a similar chain was around her waist. The final additions were the rings on her fingers. On her left she had a complex set of rings that included a full finger ring on the fourth finger, a larger ring on the middle finger that had a matching counterpart just under her nail, and a smaller ring on the forefinger, all of which were connected to the simple golden bracelet, and another piece that rested on the back of her hand. The diamonds glittered off this, and Dana had a flash of nerves as she realised how much money was on her right hand. On her left, she was given two much simpler rings and she again had to ask Ms François what they represented.

"That's a promise ring, to Digné," Ms François said, a slight smile cracking her serious demeanour for the first time. "It's a little tacky, sorry, but we thought it might be fun if you could flash it a bit." For the first time, Dana noticed the distinctive "D" logo of Digné on the ring and she grinned back.

"That works for me," she smiled. "What about the other one?" On the same ring finger of her right hand was another ring that seemed to be made of two parts with a gap between them and a complex design above it in which sat a diamond.

"That's a…" Ms François paused for a moment as she tried to choose her words. "A friendship ring," she decided upon. "It has a sister – Millie will be wearing it. It would be great if at some point you could get a picture of the two rings together. The design is complete then."

"A friendship ring?" Dana said, raising her eyebrow and giving a smirk.

"Of course. All friends with Digné," Ms François said lamely, but Dana just laughed.

"Excuse me, Miss Spectra, we have to leave," said a tall Korean man in a dark suit. "We have to get you to the concert," he explained.

"Oh yeah, of course. Oh gosh, we have to hurry," Dana said, seeing the time.

"It's fine," Ms François said. "We're running to schedule. But we leave now."

"Right," Dana agreed. To her surprise she saw the Korean man hold out his arm and Dana looked confused for a moment, wondering if

she should link arms, but Ms François rescued her by taking her right
hand and placing it on the man's arm.

"Dam Hoon will look after you," Ms François assured her. And
Dam led her to the exit.

VII

Dana Spectra discovered why no one was particularly concerned about
the trip to G'Star's concert. Their performance was in the Olympic Hall,
a concert hall in Olympic Park which was a quick drive. In fact it took
about ten minutes to get to Bangi-dong, one of the neighbourhoods in
Songpa-gu, the largest district in Seoul, and also home to Sincheon-dong,
the neighbourhood in which Lotte World Tower stood. As such, Dam
Hoon, a man who Dana had come to think of as a human brick, had
essentially become her minder and drove her to their destination quickly
and without a lot of conversation. Dana was able to discover that the man
was 42, and the father of two small children. He also admitted that his
step-daughter, a girl in her mid-teens, was actually a huge fan of Dana.
At this, when the traffic flow came to a halt, Dana had taken his phone
and snapped a selfie of the pair to send to Dam's daughter.

Olympic Park had been built in 1988 for the Seoul Summer
Olympics, in the largest and most populous district of the city. There are
two subway stations that give good access, though the most impressive
entry point is the World Peace Gate, designed by Kim Chung-up and
built in the two years leading up to the opening of the Park. The gate

consists of four pillars supporting two wings which have a stunning mural entitled *The Painting of Four Spirits*. An eternal flame sits at the centre of the pillars, calling for peace and harmony to the world. Sadly, Dana only saw this as Dam drove past on Wiryseong-daero. Given the four lanes on the highway going in the opposite direction, she was barely able to see the entrance, let alone the flame.

Having turned left into Yangjae-daero, traffic started to become a little more obstinate, and Dam was patient with the drivers around him, though Dana watched as those around them changed lanes without indicating (though, rather strangely, they would sometimes indicate an apology). Dam himself seemed to have no problem switching lanes on the journey without giving a proper indication and the speed limit seemed to be very much a guide. Actually entering the park though East Gate 2 left Dana slightly breathless, as Dam seemed to override the traffic rules in order to do so, and got a couple of severe honks from those around him. Nonetheless, no one seemed seriously put out and certainly the police didn't seem particularly interested in interfering.

Once inside, Dam made another left turn, and then another, driving the car past a large open-air venue that Dam informed Dana was for tennis. Moments later, he was pulling the car to the side, where people were milling around and several white merchandising stores had been erected. When Dam came around and opened the door for her, Dana stepped out into a series of bright flashes.

They were directly in front of the hall itself, a massive white building with a sloping roof, and over the glass entry way was a giant banner heralding G'Star – the four faces of the members painted in gold and staring out like goddesses watching over their subjects. Security guards had come forward to clear a path for Dana, and those standing around took out their phones to snap their own pictures. Dana made sure to raise her left hand to her neck, making the Digné pieces obvious in all the photos and she paused to smile and wave. To her surprise, people were thrusting pictures towards her with sharpies, and Dana realised they wanted her autograph.

Not for the first time in her life, Dana was struck with imposter syndrome, knowing full well she was simply copying those she had seen on tv and in paparazzi photos. As she made her way through the crowd toward the entrance, pausing to sign and take selfies, she kept her hand on Dam's arm as she had done the previous night with the other minder. She felt her stomach lurch slightly as the nerves struck her. This was unlike anything she had ever been through before in her life. Being photographed was simple, even signing autographs at little events was fairly straightforward. But this…this was something completely different. She had no idea if they were interested in her, rescuing a cat, falling from a tower, suddenly friends with an up-and-coming pop sensation, or simply because she was wearing hundreds of thousands of dollars' worth of jewellery. Whatever it was, the press was keen, and that made the bystanders equally as keen.

Once inside, Dana was ushered through the lobby, with Dam handing paper over to the security guards, who then passed it on to a person who was clearly some sort of usher, and from there, they were led straight into the hall.

Olympic Hall itself is an ovular shape, with one end housing the stage, and the rest of the room holding seating. There seemed to be three sets of seating – an "upper" section that ran around the room, a "lower" section that sat in front of it, and a "middle" section erected on the blue portion of the floor. The building wasn't as big as some places she had seen, and Dana was briefly taken back to Théâtre d'Apollo where the Miss Green Earth pageant had been held. It seemed to be about the same size, but not the same shape.

Dam Hoon led Dana down the aisle on the blue section, taking her towards the stage where, in the front row, were two empty seats. She was obviously a little way back from the stage, but to be that close to any stage was utterly incredible. As she sat down, the man beside her turned and gave a small bow of his head, which Dana mirrored, and this seemed to domino down the line a little. Dam leant forward and whispered: "More of our - of Digné's staff." Dana nodded, suddenly understanding that this section must have been bought by Digné even before she had been unexpectedly added to the roster. Millie's appearance was all important, and was going to bring Digné a lot of new business.

A slight tap on her shoulder caused Dana to turn, and behind her was a man in his late twenties, with dyed blue hair fashionably sculptured into a flowing mane, and dark brown eyes. His appearance sparked a memory and Dana realised this was the man who had drawn the attention at Lotte Tower earlier that day.

"Dana?" he asked in perfect English. "Dana Spectra?"

"Yes?" she nodded.

"I'm Boom," he said with a smile.

"Oh, of course, yes," Dana nodded, full of understanding thanks to Bella's K-Pop briefing.

"I'm a huge fan. Did you get my flowers?" Boom gushed, and Dana felt her cheeks go warm, but wasn't given a chance to answer. "You're a fascinating person. And so beautiful. You and Millie are great choices," he continued and for a moment Dana wondered what he meant.

"Oh thanks," she replied, and brought her hand up to display the jewellery, though even to her it seemed an odd thing to do.

"I hope we can talk later?"

"That would be amazing," Dana replied, but the conversation was cut off as the lights dimmed. Dana smiled apologetically and turned back, noticing Dan was scowling.   She briefly wondered why but then the stage seemed to sparkle and lights in different shades of yellow and orange flicked over it, while on giant screens at the back of the stage, the glitter seemed to be forming into faces – the four faces of G'Star.

Around her, the strains of the music started to float and strange, discordant harmonies reached across the rooms, silencing everyone. As the lights dimmed, four explosions seemed to take place on stage, and when they cleared, the four members of G'Star stood. To the left was Amy, dressed in a golden coat with black shorts and a black crop top, her hair a golden bob. Beside her, Mee, with her long blonde hair, was dressed in tight little gold dress with long black boots. Then was Millie, her short black hair now spiky and golden tipped, was in golden hot pants and a short, midriff coat with long tails. Finally, on the far end, her long, dark hair blowing in the wind of some fan that must have been off-stage, was Soojin. Her soft features were framed by a golden tiara, while a long, flowing gold top swirled around her, looking a little like a mini-dress.

When the music started up again, Amy's rap belted out and *Epic* began.

Throughout the performance Dana took some footage with her phone and snapped photos, sending them back to Bella, gushing over the show. G'Star's music flowed through her, sending her mind to a variety of places, thanks to Mee's light girly voice, Soojin's husky tones, Amy's growling rap and Millie's whispering vocals in both rap and melody. They were a unique ensemble, and their music was enthralling. At one point Dam passed her a box in which was a black stick with a clear top that lit up gold when she pressed the button on the side. All around her in the Hall, fans were carrying similar light sticks and in the dark the dots of white and gold created a glittery effect that complimented the lighting on stage.

As ridiculous as it seemed, between the magnetic sounds and mesmerising lights, Dana felt like she was falling in love with the group. All thoughts of what had happened earlier in the day were completely gone. She was genuinely Glitter.

VIII

Immediately after the encore and people started to flood out of the Hall, Dam Hoon proffered his arm and Dana took it, but not before bowing to the other Digné staff that were to her left. Boom had already disappeared, to Dana's surprise. Guided by Dam Hoon to one of the side doors near the stage, the security guards there opened the door to give them access to backstage. They were taken down the side corridors where backstage crew hustled back and forth on their way to check equipment and ensure that everything was shut down. The staff of the Olympic Hall had their fill for the night and were keen to get out and go home. Very few people paid any attention to Dana as she was escorted by Dam down the corridors.

When they came to the green room, Dana was not entirely surprised to see that Ms François was already there, looking a little edgy. She said something in French which Dana didn't quite catch, but as she glanced at her watch, Dana suspected that they were waiting for the rest of G'Star to make an appearance – or perhaps more accurately, just Millie.

As Soojin stepped out of the doorway that led to the dressing room, Ms François leapt into action and grabbed Dana by the elbow to lead her to an opposite door. Dana looked a little puzzled, but was curiously reassured to see Dam Hoon right behind her, and as she was led out of the door she found herself in the outside world, though clearly Digné had prepared this for *the* moment.

Photographers were already there and Ms François gave Dana a little nod – go do your thing, girl. With her left hand back against her throat, Dana stepped forward to allow herself to be photographed. Out of the corner of her eye she saw a girl in a short black dress carrying a tray of drinks, and Dana wondered if it would be inappropriate to grab one as quickly as possible.

This inclination was certainly not swayed by the bombardment of questions that were being fired at her, which ranged from the simple ("Did you enjoy the concert?") to the obvious ("Do you feel becoming an ambassador for Digné is a highlight of your career?") to the awkward ("Is it too soon for you to be out after someone tried to murder you this morning?") Most of the questions were in English, but Dam whispered to her when they came in Korean and even Ms François supplied a translation when someone snapped out something in French.

Dana looked around to see if she could see Boom, but he was nowhere in sight. However, Dana thought she saw someone familiar in the crowd – an androgynous face with short, white blonde hair.

"Hi there. Mason Lemon, nice to meet you." Dana turned to see who was talking to her, but when she looked back, white-blonde had disappeared. Puzzled, Dana turned back to talk to the American who had introduced himself.

The conversations with journalists seemed to take an eternity, but in fact later Dana realised that Ms François' planning was impressively well timed as Soojin's appearance in the green room obviously heralded the arrival of the rest of G'Star, and sure enough the group stepped out of the exit, stealing away some of Dana's publicity.

Millie had walked up to Dana, and for the first time Dana realised that the girl was about the same height as she was. Both in heels now, Millie was wearing stockings with a Cettire sleeveless tartan dress in white. Millie's silver jewellery gave the impression that she was the moon and Dana was the sun, which caused Dana to genuinely smile at the skill of Mainard Descoteaux and his launch. Millie slid her arm around Dana's waist and the model reciprocated causing a swell of flashes. Millie's usually serious face had become more playful, almost flirty. Dana suddenly remembered that Bella had described G'Star as one of the Girl Crush K-Pop bands – groups that embraced the power of being women and were aspirational. Dana slid her hand into Millie's, who gripped it, and the two stood in what Dana hoped would make them look a little like superheroes. This had the desired effect of generating more photos and questions were again shouted at the two girls.

At some point the rest of G'Star joined the two, and Dana realised she had lost all track of time, not sure how long she had been answering questions or posing for, but for the first time she was actually enjoying the entire process. Amy and Soojin introduced themselves, the former having as much energy as Mee, bouncing over and bowing before Dana embraced her, and Soojin bowed far more officially before offering her hand and smiling. Mee whispered in her ear that Soojin didn't have particularly good English and as such was more reserved about conversing with Dana, who had no Korean at all.

Nonetheless at some point the woman in the dark suit from the night before, with the iPad wielding assistant, again stepped forward to start issuing instructions to her staff and to inform Ms François of what G'Star was about to do. The French woman didn't seem remotely concerned, and when she flashed a smile for the first time at Dana, Dana realised that the evening had played out the way she had planned. The media attention was exactly what Digné wanted and at that point everything was satisfactory.

The woman in the dark suit signalled to the G'Star's staff, and they started to move the girls off towards a waiting car. Soojin suddenly said something and spoke quickly to the other members of G'Star. Millie stepped away from the group, heading over to Dana and took her hand.

"Do you want to come back to our place and celebrate tonight?" she asked, her face having resumed its neutral expression.

"Oh, you guys probably want to do stuff…" Dana said, but Millie shook her head.

"We want you to come. Even Soojin. She wants to get to know you. We have tomorrow off, and we can't go out because of the rules."

"The rules?"

"Our company has strict rules, remember. No nightclubs. But we can celebrate. You should come with us." Dana paused, feeling the other girl's hand in hers, and suddenly she was back in the concert, the music and the movements filling her head.

"Of course," she whispered. Millie took her hand and drew her back into G'Star's world.

IX

The journey from Olympic Hall took place via the spacious Genesis GV80 that G'Star had travelled to. Dana had no idea where they were going, or really even how long the journey was – all she noticed was that they crossed the river Han twice. In truth the atmosphere inside the car was far more exciting, as all four members of G'Star were still hyped about their performance, and with the omnipresent cameras no longer on them, they were allowed to cut loose, turning the music in the car up (not their own, but rather other groups like (G)I-dle, Blackpink and Itzy), singing along and laughing at their own jokes. Even the typically dour Millie was far more relaxed. At one point Amy had turned to one of their managers and asked if they could stop off for alcohol, but he gave her a severe look, and she stuck her tongue at him, before bursting into laughter and falling back onto the chair, almost in Mee's lap.

Dana noticed that away from the cameras, the four girls relationships were subtly different. Their friendship was obvious and shone through to the world of the stage, but behind closed doors there was a chemistry between Mee and Amy that suggested something far more intimate, as they barely let each other go. Dana wondered if she was reading too much into it, but Soojin and Millie seemed indulgent, which suggested there was something to indulge. She guessed that the managers were aware but chose to do nothing about it. As long as it didn't go public, Dana suspected that Moonlight would be happy. Though striving for more equality for the LGBTQ community, South Korea still wasn't at a point where they would be happy for their idols to reveal anything scandalous.

The car slowed, and Dana leaned forward to get a better look at their destination – three massive towers linked by a walkway around the middle of the smallest tower. The car jerked and Dana fell forward into Millie's arms who giggled and both Amy and Mee pulled her back, though Millie grabbed at Dana's arms and pulled her forward, causing another eruption of laughter at the human tug-of-war.
Dana finally slumped back between the two younger girls, breaking them

apart.

"Where are we?" she asked.

"Raemian Caelitus," Soojin answered, surprising Dana a little. Soojin had barely spoken much to Dana, and though she seemed distant, Dana guessed it might be because the older girl didn't have a strong grasp on English. "We live there," she grinned.

"It's very private," Amy said into her ear.

The driver had come off Gangbyeonbuk-ro and driven around Ichon-ro, before turning down the street that gave access to Raemian Caelitus and its carpark, which the Genesis easily turned into without stopping, the boom gate opening, presumably in response to a signal from something in the car.

Once the car had been parked, the women all piled out of the car and G'Star headed straight to a set of elevators, dragging Dana behind them. The smell of concrete and diesel brought Dana back to Earth, as all the excitement of earlier, with the myriad of scents from the smells of Olympic Park, the fragrances that everyone had been wearing and the aroma of the food that was being offered, was swept away by the mundanity of everyday living. It may have been for a very expensive apartment block, but a carpark was a carpark regardless of who you were with.

The elevator doors opened and the girls entered, with their managers and Dam Hoon keeping up behind them.

"They aren't coming with, are they?" Dana giggled a little, and all four popstars laughed with her.

"No, just to see us into our rooms so we aren't disturbed and then they'll go home and leave us be," Mee grinned. "They're very protective. It's so nice."

"But so unnecessary here," Millie pointed out.

The men remained solemn-faced, and Dana realised that she hadn't even taken time out to see who they were. They had just become faceless bodyguards. She felt slightly ashamed of herself for being that way, and she touched Dam on the arm and said thank you. He smiled at her, though his fellows remained unmoved.

G'Star's apartment was in tower two on the 31st floor, and was comfortably one of the most luxurious apartments Dana had ever seen. Large and spacious, the most noticeable thing about it was the floor-to-ceiling windows that looked over the Han River, though from the other side of where Dana would have been viewing at the Signiel. The floors were all wood panelled, with elegant lighting set into recesses in the ceiling. The kitchen was a little more cramped that Dana would have expected, but with the open plan of the majority of the apartment, it still seemed large. Soojin had immediately turned on the big black television that hung from the wall and slumped down onto a couch opposite that was large and pink and not only looked a little like a mouth, but threatened to swallow the K-Pop star up. Millie had gone to the fridge and opened it to reveal that alcohol had not been necessary. With music now pumping out of the television, Millie supplied the other option, pressing a beer bottle into her hand which had a distinctive blue and white label. Millie tossed one over to Soojin who caught it with practiced ease and flipped off the top to start drinking. Millie glanced around the room, and Dana followed her eyes to see that Amy and Mee were too busy giggling and holding hands.

"Hey! Beer, you two!" Millie called out, and the two turned and let loose another burst of giggles, before coming over. "Take your coat off and get comfortable," Millie continued, talking to Dana. Dana nodded and shrugged off the Angel Chen jacket.   She looked around and Millie pointed to the dining table, where Dana deposited the jacket and also took the phone out of her bum pocket and slid it into the yellow material. The jacket caught on her hand as she took it off, and so she also popped her bag on the table and took off the ear rings, rings, necklace, bracelet and hand piece from Digné, and slid them into the bag.

"Good idea," enthused Millie, removing her pieces and dumping them into Dana's bag as well. "You can give that back to them from me," she grinned. "Saves me the trip."

"You're very talkative all of a sudden," Dana teased, poking the Korean girl in the side.

"Very excited from the concert. I'm…what's the word?" Millie paused, grasping for a word that was clearly lost in the multilingual vocabulary bank in her head.

"Hyped?"

"Yeah, hyped," grinned Millie.

"How many languages do you guys actually speak?" Dana wondered aloud, suddenly realising that finding the correct words in any one language would be a frequent problem.

"Korean fluently. Pretty good English and Japanese," answered

Millie.

"Amazing Japanese!" called out Amy from the couch where she and Mee had fallen on, beside Soojin.

"Chinese," added Soojin.

"But no English," Mee giggled, turning to Soojin, who glared at her and smacked her hand. The energy of the four was extraordinary, Dana mused, and wondered what on Earth they were going to be like when they were drunk as well.

X

Any concerns Dana had were tossed out the door as she got as sloshed as the idols. The music belted out, and they danced and sang and behaved like fools simply because they could. At one point when the music took on a seductive and sexy tone, Dana pushed Mee onto the couch and pushed her legs apart, as though to start of a strip tease. The Asian girls all burst into laughter, and gave a loud "ooo!" as Dana sat on Mee's lap. When the doorbell rang, however, the mood immediately changed and all four idols suddenly looked at each other guiltily.

The hierarchy took control, though, and Soojin immediately leapt up, mumbling an apology as she bumped into Dana and raced to the door. There was a modern doorbell on it, and Soojin pressed a button bringing the little screen to life to show who was outside the door. To Dana's surprise she immediately recognised Boom, and she was even more surprised when Soojin appeared to breathe a sigh of relief and opened the door. Standing with his traditional swagger, Boom remained framed in the doorway until Soojin pulled him in and closed the door. Before she could go any further, Boom grabbed her and pushed her up against the wall to kiss her. Dana's mouth dropped, but she had little time to think as Millie had pulled the model onto the chair beside her.

"Don't worry," whispered Millie. "He and Soojin have been an item ever since he joined Moonlight. She got him in, actually."

"Really?"

"Yeah, it was a bit wild. The first non-Korean guy in Moonlight."

"He's not Korean?" Dana asked, curiously.

"Boom is short for Boon-mee. Boon-mee Sirisopa. There's not a lot of non-Koreans at all, really. Just a Thai and a Japanese girl," she added with a wink.

"Oh, and a North Korean," Amy rejoined playfully. Dana couldn't quite place the series of reactions, but she knew that Amy's comment made it clear that Millie was North Korean, and after Karim's discussion, she definitely reacted. Millie's response was even more intense, but whether it was to Amy's comment or Dana's reaction, Dana wasn't sure. Either way, Millie managed to get up, forcing Dana to fall to one side of the couch, and left the room, her arms wrapped around herself.

Soojin had noticed and walked up to the younger girls, speaking quickly to them in Korean. Boom said something as well, but Soojin replied and waved her hand at the same time, while the younger girls sat chastened, but saying nothing. Soojin said something again, and then looked at Dana and in her stilted English said, "I so sorry." With that she turned and grabbed Boom, leading him into one of the doors around the lounge.

Totally confused, Dana turned to the younger girls, and they both got up and came and sat on either side of Dana.

"I shouldn't have said that," Amy said softly, her head low. "Please don't tell anyone that Millie is a defector."

"She's a refugee?"

"She and her father escaped North Korea ages ago. They ended up in China and then came to Seoul," Mee explained. "No one knows that Millie is North Korean outside of us and maybe some of the Moonlight executives. Definitely no Glitter. It can't get out. Even Boom doesn't know, and Soojin is going to make sure he heard nothing." She took Dana's hands. "Please." To her surprise, Amy took her hands as well.

"I've been a terrible person," whispered Amy. "I know we barely know you, and we just got carried away and we've all been stupid. Normally we do this when it's just us so it doesn't matter. It's so wrong to ask this of you…"

"It's fine," Dana said, squeezing both sets of hands. "Honestly I promise. I won't tell anyone. It's got nothing to do with me. And it's not an issue for me. I promise you." She squeezed their hands again, and the two members look relieved.

"I'll go talk to Millie," Mee said.

"No, I will," Dana reassured her. "You guys go back to being you. I'll make sure Millie knows I'm not going to destroy her life." The two singers looked uncertain, but when Dana squeezed their hands again they gave a visible sigh of relief. The model hopped up and set off after Millie. Halfway across the room, she turned back to see the girls looking at her, cautiously. "Get back to it," she grinned, and Mee smiled in understanding, grabbing her friend's hands.

Millie had gone down a corridor past the kitchen, so Dana wasn't entirely certain which room she had gone into, but she could hear something from one of the rooms, and she pushed open the door to catch Millie in nothing but her g-string.

"Oh, god, I'm so sorry," Dana said, backing out.

"It's OK," replied Millie, her hand across her chest. "You can come in." She paused for a moment, and then turned and grabbed a t-shirt which she pulled on, though it just covered her boobs.

"I just wanted to tell you I'm not going to tell anyone your secret," Dana started. "I promise. It has nothing to do with me. But I don't know why you're worried." Millie's face remained blank, but there was a slight twist of her mouth when Dana finished.

"You're not Korean," Millie said. "If you were, you'd have something to say about where I come from. Trust me, they all do."

"Surely not all," replied Dana, but then shut her mouth, realising she had no experience of what the other girl had been through, and really had no right to say anything. To her surprise, however, Millie sat down beside her.

"No," she agreed, "not all. Those girls out there have never judged me or hated me. They treat me like a sister. They're my family and I love them so much. When they found out they just embraced me, and I hoped and prayed that when Moonlight formed a girl group I would be with them. But others…" She paused and shook her head, remembering. "People have been so cruel. My father…" She was unable to continue, and Dana reached across and took her hand, which Millie accepted. "So many people hate us because we are North Korean. We didn't have a choice. We didn't want to be there ever. It was horrible. Getting away from there…I don't remember much because I was really young, but I know my father didn't limp before we left. And I know I had a mother before we did."

"I'm so sorry," Dana whispered, appalled.

"I'm not evil. I was just born in the wrong place." There was silence, and Dana felt ashamed of herself for even buying into Karim's suspicions. On a whim she reached out and took her fellow Ambassador's hand and they sat in silence, with just the moon gazing upon them.

XI

Dana glanced blearily at the clock that shone brightly, the back of her mind somewhere taking in the fact that it read 3.14. In the morning, she guessed, noting that she was in darkness. Her arm was across a body and as she turned her head, she smiled a little seeing the face of Millie beside her, her short hair spiky from sleep, and drool coming from her mouth. Dana removed her arm carefully, and as her eyes accustomed to the dark she took in the details of the room she was in. They had sat in silence, and then laid back and talked. Somewhere in that, Dana realised she was fading in and out, and there was a point when she thought Millie had fallen asleep, but she assumed she had followed, because she couldn't remember anything much beyond that.

Dana stood up and padded softly to the door, sliding it open and stepping into the corridor. She needed water and she realised that she had woken because she needed to pee. The water shouldn't have been particularly difficult to find, but the toilet, that was another thing. She hadn't actually bothered to look beyond the communal area when she had entered the spacious apartment.

She walked to the doorway opposite and slid it back, but realised she had made a mistake. Two naked bodies, glistening with sweat, were sprawled out on the bed in front of her. Dana shook her head slightly and wondered how often concerts around the world ended up in this state. Probably quite a few, she reflected. Music seemed to cover all the common ground.

She made her way into the communal area, grabbing a clean cup from the neatly ordered stack on the shelf above the sink, and poured water into it from the cold water dispenser on the fridge. Then she set off down the opposite corridor, sipping at her beverage.

Another door revealed another bedroom, unused, while the next door was another naked G'Star member – this time the perfect Soojin, in much the same state as the other girls; vulnerably just herself.

Where the fuck was the toilet?

There was another door at the end of the corridor, but when Dana opened that it was just an empty room with musical instruments laying about. Surely this girls must use the toilet at some point, she thought, a little annoyed. As she headed back, she realised she hadn't shut Soojin's door properly, but then she noticed the sliver of light near the back of the room, and with a little astonishment at her own stupidity, Dana realised that each room would have its own en suite.

Feeling utterly stupid, she pondered about heading back to the corridor to use Millie's or ducking into the empty room, which became her path of choice. Having relieved herself, she headed back to Millie's room to finish her sleep, but as she did, she passed the dining room table and her Angel Chen yellow coat, which prompted her to get her mobile.

As she did, the jacket slid, and Dana tried to catch her handbag from falling off.

Except it didn't.

It wasn't there.

Almost like a switch, Dana became alert, and she scanned the table, grabbing her phone at the same time so she could use the torch to give a better view. The bag, however, was assuredly not there.

"Fuck," murmured Dana, as she flashed the torch around, scanning the room. However, there was obstinately no sign of the bag. Dana could feel herself getting physically sick as the implications of what might have happened began to sink in. She began pulling the cushions off the couch to make sure there was no sign of the bag. "Oh fuck," she said, a little louder this time.

"Hey, you'll get cold," came a voice behind her, and Dana spun to see Millie, wrapped in a robe, but Dana shook her head and turned back to the table. "What have I done?"

"The bag has gone," Dana hissed.

"I don't understand," Millie said, confused.

"The bag," repeated Dana. "The one with the Digné jewellery in. It's gone!" Whether it was the urgency in her voice, or simply the same implications that had hit Dana earlier, Millie's face immediately changed, and she quickly went over and activated the huge overhead lights, illuminating the communal area. Despite covering the same ground, she joined Dana's search, but they soon returned the same results.

At this point, however, they had attracted the attention of the other girls who had woken up and staggered out. Like Millie, they were all wearing dressing gowns, whether a practical, woollen gown like Millie's, or a skimpy, modesty protector like Mee's.

"What's up?" Mee asked, the same bleariness that Dana had earlier in her voice. Millie replied in Korean and alarm crossed the faces of the other three girls.

"You should cover in case Boom sees you," Soojin said to Dana, taking her arm, but as she did, Dana snapped around to look at her.

"Boom?"

"My boyfriend," she replied in stilted English.

"I know who he is," Dana growled. "Where is he?" Soojin

looked puzzled and then realised what Dana had also worked out –
Boom hadn't been in her room. Without waiting for a response, Dana
turned and stormed down to Millie's room, grabbing any of her garments
that had been lost earlier in the night. By the time Millie followed, Dana
had already got her clothes on.

"What are you doing?" she asked.

"He's taken the jewellery," Dana snarled, and strode from the
room to the communal area to get her jeans.

"No," protested Millie following. "He wouldn't."

"Why?" Dana said, turning so fast Millie almost walked into
her.

"He's…Soojin's boyfriend," Millie replied meekly.

"He's not here," Amy said, and Dana turned to see the other
three were in the room as well.

"When did he leave?" Dana asked, turning on Soojin.

"Hey," Amy said, grabbing her arm. "Don't be mean." Dana
turned to her, ready to fight, but instead drew a deep breath. She bowed
her head to Amy and then to Soojin.

"I'm very sorry," she said, "but I'm terrified. If I've lost the
jewellery…"

"We," Millie said, touching her on the shoulder. "We lost it. You
don't have to do this alone."

"We'll help in any way we can," Mee assured her. Dana paused,
and thought she was going to burst into tears, but Mee did it for her
instead, and to Dana's surprise the others gathered around her, embracing

her. Even more surprising, Soojin grabbed her and pulled her in. The truth of Millie's earlier words about them being a close-knit family hit home and Dana let the tears flow a little.

"I didn't know he had left," Soojin said, as she held the embrace, and Dana again took a deep breath and got back control. This was no time to cry.

"Do you know where he lives?" Dana asked.

"Just downstairs," Amy replied.

"I show you," said Soojin, her English becoming more stilted in proportion to her stress, and she dashed back to her room. Her change was quick, and she was at the door with Dana even as the group hug ended. Soojin pulled the front door open and she and Dana stepped out, but as they did, Dana looked up and down the corridor.

"Where's Dam?" she asked.

"He must have gone home," Soojin said. Dana narrowed her eyes, unconvinced, but Soojin was already heading towards the lifts.

They headed down to the next level, and Dana continued to follow Soojin, who led her to a room and then typed in a code on the side of the door. Once they were inside the apartment – which was smaller than the one G'Star owned, but given that it only serviced one person instead of four, was arguably much more grandiose – Dana knew she should have been surprised to see Dam Hoon lying on the floor, blood pooling around his body, but a part of her knew that she would find the man like this. There was clearly a bullet hole in his chest, which meant that Boom had lived up to his name and was already armed. Dana pulled the man's coat open and saw a taser tucked into a holster on the belt, which she removed, as well as a set of car keys. Rather more depressingly she found his wallet, inside which was a picture of his two young children.

Soojin was rooted to the spot, her hand to her mouth. Dana looked around the room, and quickly went down the corridor, mentally noting that the layout of the apartment was not dissimilar to the one upstairs, though with only one corridor, and therefore half the rooms. There was no sign of Boom, who had clearly left the building, taking his earnings with him. Yet he had come back here, because Dam had followed him, obviously suspicious about what he was taking. Once inside the room, Boom had access to his firearm which gave him the upper hand.

She crossed over to the kitchen where there was a plastic container of brake fluid. When she approached it, the smell of fish oil became more obvious and as she sniffed at the top of the container it was even more apparent.

"Son of a bitch," she murmured, remembering the smell from the SkyBridge.

The only problem now was, what was she going to do? She had no idea where Boom might have gone, and he had left no obvious trail that she could tell. All she had was her taser and phone, and neither of those were going to give her Boom's location.

Or could they?

She took out her phone and placed her little finger on the small red dot in the top corner, and as demonstrated earlier, her phone went black before rebooting with a new interface. Dana looked at the apps that were available to her and to her delight she saw one marked "Phone Trace".

"Soojin, do you know Boom's number?" The Korean girl looked at her confused, and Dana held up her phone. "His telephone number?"

"Oh, yes, yes! 011 4820 2791," she read from her phone, and Dana tapped the app and typed the number in. To her surprise the phone started to ring, and the girls stood transfixed as they wondered what was going to happen.

"*Nuguseyo?*" came Boom's voice, and Soojin gasped, but Dana clapped her hand over the other girl's mouth. "Hello?"

Dana's heart pounded in her chest, but she kept her hand over Soojin's mouth and watched the screen of her phone. A map had appeared and a large circle appeared over what was clearly Seoul. The circle got smaller and smaller as Boom said "Ahh!"

Terrified that he was about to hang up, Dana coughed and it was enough to catch Boom's attention. "*Nuguseyo??*" he demanded again, but the circle had now gotten as small as it was going to, changing from the shadowy black it had been to a pointed red. Dana disconnected the phone and found a specific longitude and latitude had been given on the map. Dana copied it, and closed the app, finding a map app that allowed her to plug her copied information into, and within seconds there was a neat red line leading from Raemian Caelitus to where Boom was currently hiding.

"What are you going to do?" Soojin asked, touching Dana on the arm.

"I'm going after him. He's taken the jewellery, and we need it back."

"But," though before Soojin could continue, Dana pointed to the corpse of Dam Hoon.

"This has gone way too far, Soojin," Dana said softly, not without compassion. A sudden gasp made her look up and she saw Amy was standing in the doorway, clearly shocked about the dead bodyguard.

"Amy, take Soojin back to your apartment," Dana instructed. She guided Soojin out of the room, and Amy linked her arm with the older girl's. "You lot stay here. I'm going to get the jewellery back," Dana explained.

"You can't do it alone," whispered Amy. "Call the police. They will help."

"I think it's better if we handle this in house," Dana said with a slight grimace. As they approached the elevator, Dana saw that both Millie and Mee were standing there, and like Amy they were all dressed casually. "Look after each other," instructed Dana. "I promise I won't be too long."

"You'll need your coat," said Millie, and Dana suddenly realised that Millie had been wearing it.

"Thanks," Dana grinned. She leaned forward and embraced Millie, before doing the same to the other three girls. "It's going to be fine," she promised. "Trust me."

"How do you know," Mee began, but Dana put her finger to her lips.

"You really don't want to know."

The elevator arrived, but it was heading down, so Dana stepped inside it. "Look after each other," she repeated, and the let the doors slide shut.

XII

Dana drove the Genesis SUV through the streets of Korea, with a fierce intensity until several things began to hit her. Firstly, the traffic was very limited, which was probably not surprising for the time of morning, but it might mean that she would be a target for the Korean police, if she was doing the wrong thing. And that would be a problem because she suddenly realised she probably wasn't allowed to drive in Korea. She certainly didn't have a Korean licence, and the less said about her blood-alcohol level, the better.

She was already a little worried, given that when she had started the car, there had been a curious bump, and Dana briefly panicked, thinking she had reversed into another car. It was, however, a moot point. She had to find Boom – that was her main priority. She could deal with the other details later.

Dana couldn't help but give a wry smile as her map displayed a number of names that were immediately familiar to her. She was heading into the Gangnam district, and her map picked out a number of buildings that exploring the K-pop world had exposed her to. SM Entertainment and JYP Entertainment both had their headquarters near to where she was driving. Gangnam was an affluent district of Seoul, and even as she crossed Yeongdong Bridge, she could see that the traffic was starting to build up a little.

Her phone was sending her along Yeongdong-Daero, a street filled with the traditional buildings most big cities were made from, glass and concrete separated only from the rest of the world by the Hangeul on them. Having passed a Tesla storefront and two hospitals, Dana pulled to a quick stop when she realised her phone was indicating she had reached her destination. Her aberrant driving didn't attract any undue attention and deciding to risk something that might get her into trouble, she pulled into the nearest carpark which was out the front of a hospital, recognisable only by the red cross on the front.

As she stepped out of the car, her phone map zoomed in on the area she was supposed to be, and gave her a more precise path to walk – in fact right next door where a three story glass building stood, utterly empty. Utterly empty except for the man with the sullen features and the dark suit standing at the front. He stared impassively ahead of him, guarding the doorway behind him, which was odd given the building seemed to have nothing in it.

Who puts a guard on an empty building?

It wasn't unheard of, Dana supposed, but she had a weird sense that something was wrong.

She glanced around, taking in her surroundings properly for the first time. Most of Seoul tended to light up like a Christmas tree at night, but Yeongdeong-Daero was sleepy, though Dana wasn't sure whether that just happened to be the time of night or not. The air was cold, something which hit Dana for the first time since her arrival. It was winter in Korea and at 3 in the morning it was freezing. No longer pumping adrenaline, Dana felt the cold starting to bite, particularly around her exposed legs. She was suddenly very grateful that Millie had given her the jacket, not least because it also gave her a place to hide her taser.

Dana Spectra pondered on her options, whilst her phone resolutely pointed towards the glass building. Chewing her bottom lip, she guessed that she could maybe try to find an alternative entry point, but that could be difficult, and who knows how much time she had – after all she had no idea what Boom was doing in the building. Screwing up her courage, she decided to go for the front door approach.

She strolled casually up to the security guard who initially didn't give her a second glance, but when she was standing right beside him, he turned to regard her with a fair degree of dispassion.

"Hi," Dana smiled. "Uhm, I was wondering what was going on in there." She pointed to the revolving door behind him, but the guard just raised an eyebrow and turned to face the front again. Dana took a step toward the door, but the guard's hand was in front of her, making it clear she was not to go in. He even deigned to look at her again, this time shaking his head slowly.

Dana nodded, and felt the taser in her pocket.

"Sorry," she said. "I just…oh what's that?" She pointed up the street, and was genuinely astonished when the guard turned to look at what she was pretending to point at. Quickly she whipped out the taser and jabbed it in the guard's neck, activating it. Ozone sizzled and the man literally shook in front of her, before collapsing to the ground. Dana quickly searched the guard, looking around to see if anyone had seen anything, but the darkness seemed to have kept her actions hidden from view. She paused for a moment when she thought she saw someone, but when she blinked, she realised she was alone.

Needing a weapon to give her an edge (given that it was clear Boom was also packing), she searched the guard and gave a slight smirk when she found a gun – a shining grey Colt M1911, with a bright red grip. The guard started to groan, recovering from the electricity that had coursed through his body, so Dana swiftly headed to the revolving door and pushed her way into the building. She slid the gun into her waistband in the small of her back, feeling it tug down on her jeans sitting there a little uncomfortably, but she didn't let it bother her. Unless they were about to fall off, she could live with the awkwardness.

Inside, the building was large and empty, and Dana wondered if it had perhaps been a car showroom at some point. There didn't seem to be any activity coming from the floors above, so she moved forward into the darkness, trying to find something that might lead below. When she passed a door, she felt a hum of activity behind it, a faint vibration of sound or electricity. She turned the handle and it easily opened into a set of stairs that did indeed lead down to another doorway, light streaming behind it and a bass line thumping.

Dana headed down the stairs and opened the door to enter, but more movement in the corner of her eye made her go through and close the door behind her. The guard had clearly followed her and was looking for her, so she banked on the fact that there was a crowd she could lose herself in.

To her surprise she had entered what appeared to be an underground casino, populated mostly by Korean nationals. She made her way around the outskirts of the casino, noting it was busy with tables and cards, well dressed croupiers flicking out cards and scantily clad barmaids bringing drinks to those that required them.

There were a few foreigners, mostly women, dressed in a variety of ways and looking ultra-cool on the arms of their Korean partners, who were dressed equally fantastically in clean suits with thin lapels, and collarless shirts. As such, Dana blended in rather nicely, and no one gave her a second look (well, they let their first look turn into a lascivious gaze, but beyond imagining her naked, they didn't cast a second glance).

As she made her way around the room, she found exactly what she was looking for – a table that was playing Texas Hold 'em, with four Korean gentleman seated, dressed in a variety of styles. One had a pale blue suit, blue hair swept to the side and a model's good looks – Boom. Cards were being laid down, and as the croupier flipped them over, Boom's smile grew.

Until the heavy-set gentleman beside him turned over his two cards. The croupier leant forward and rearranged the cards in the centre of the table, and it was clear that whether Boom had a good poker face or not, the cards had not gone his way. The heavy-set gentleman gave a belly laugh, obviously knowing that Boom's cards were ordinary, and sure enough when he flipped them over, Boom slumped back in his seat accepting defeat.

And then someone else appeared, and for a moment, Dana couldn't quite believe her eyes. Approaching the table in a svelte deep purple velvet bodysuit with high neck, no sleeves and ruffled shorts, as well as a cool black leather biker jacket was Millie. Dana's heart sunk.

Up to this point things seemed pretty obvious – Boom had stolen the jewellery and was the one who tried to kill her on the Skybridge. Karim's agitator was probably him, surely? There was certainly no reason to automatically suspect the North Korean refugee. Except they were both with Moonlight and so both had access to the people who had been killed in the past. But why was Millie here now? How did she even get here before Dana? Unless she knew where to go…

No reason to suspect the North Korean refugee, sure, if you discounted the fact she shouldn't have been here.

Millie rested her butt against the table, her long legs – made even longer by the short shorts – attracting the attention of everyone, including Boom. She placed her hand on Boom's shoulder and then made a gesture to take in the whole table. Standing in the crowd to remain unseen, Dana had no idea what they were saying, but whatever it was, it appealed to everyone except Boom, who looked annoyed, and then resigned. He shrugged his shoulders and stood up, bowing his head at the other players and then took Millie's hand in his and led her away from the table.

Quickly Dana followed, her left hand reaching to the small of her back to rest on the Colt there. Boom had got to a door, which he opened and gallantly let Millie enter. Dana sped up to get to the door before it closed shut after Boom had entered, and when she burst through, she had the gun out, ready to shoot.

Inside the room was a stack of lockers, and both Millie and Boom turned around in surprise, Boom at one of the lockers. Seeing Dana, he pulled a gun from the locker and grabbed Millie, holding the gun to her head.

"Well, well, look who is here, cobber," drawled Boom, a grin on his perfect features. "You wanna toss a shrimp on the barbie?" Millie's face had gone pale and Dana frowned a little uncertain about what exactly was going on. There was still one fact she was certain of, and that, she decided, was what she would run with.

"Where's the jewellery?" she snapped.

"In the locker," came the surprisingly honest response. "Why are you so bothered? Who gives a shit? They are insured. Digné will not mind."

"I mind," Dana replied.

"Me too," whimpered Millie.

"Let her go," demanded Dana.

"Oh, I don't think so," Boom sneered. "Whacha gonna do? You can't shoot me. You might hit her. That wouldn't look good."

Dana squeezed the trigger and the sound of the Colt going off sounded strangely loud to everyone in the room, though the shock on Boom's face made it clear he had definitely not expected her to do what she did. When he realised he hadn't been shot, however, a look of relief flooded his face.

"You missed," he grinned.

"Did I?" Dana asked innocently. Boom's puzzled features turned slightly and he saw that Dana's bullet had gone through a calendar that was on the wall behind him – directly through the centre of the 14th. When he turned back, he looked a whole lot less certain than he had before.

"It's not the 14th," he said, trying to regain some confidence.

"I'm superstitious," Dana smirked.

"I could still kill her," Boom said, but there was a little less certainty in his voice now.

Colonel Indigo Spectra had once told his daughter, when they were wandering through a rainforest looking for the rest of their family, that everyone often faced a moment where a decision needed to be taken and the heart and head would fight over what to do. If the head won, then it was as it should be. If the heart won, then that was a moment you needed to listen to yourself, because the compass of morality had been defined. When she had asked her father what that meant he had laughed and told her of the time he had been desperate to take her mother on a date. Unfortunately, his car had broken down, which meant there was no way to get to her. But, he announced with all the passion of an old school preacher, he was working for a pizza delivery company at the time and he had the opportunity to, well not steal as such, but *borrow* the company car to meet up with his girlfriend.

His head had emphatically tried to stop this from happening.

There were so many reasons why this was a bad idea, not least because no matter how often he used the word *borrow* it didn't change the fact it was nothing more than a fairly obvious pseudonym for steal. But his heart was in the driving seat and so the car was *borrowed*. That, he realised, was when the compass of his morality had been decided. One woman was more important to him than stealing a car, and so he knew he had found the love of his life.

Some months earlier, Dana had come to the very solid conclusion she wasn't a killer. She had killed, but she wasn't a killer, and she had no desire to cause the death of anyone. But she had made the decision, the choice between her heart and her head, the choice that decided *who* she was. She was many things – a sister, a daughter, a model, an animal activist, someone who drank too much on occasion, and someone who had a tendency to leap into bed with people a little too quickly. But none of those were *who* she was. She rescued Dine, the cat because it was the right thing to do, and that was the person she had decided she was. She would do the right thing, and she had to be pragmatic under those circumstances. The right thing was laid out before her. But she didn't have to take a life to do it – in fact she would actively avoid it.

But she would be pragmatic and she would do the right thing.

And she needed to have confidence in herself and her abilities.

So when she squeezed the trigger a second time, it was with the confidence she had absolutely aimed for the 14th on the calendar. It was with the confidence she would hit her target.

The bullet hit Boom in the right shoulder, causing him to

immediately drop the gun as he was spun back, and setting Millie free.

"Mother fucker," he exclaimed, grabbing his shoulder and falling to his knees.

"Get the jewellery," Dana ordered Millie, and it wasn't lost on the Korean girl that the Australian had not dropped the gun. But she kept it on Boom, and when Millie stepped up with the stash safely in her hands, Dana reached into her jean pocket and gave her a small card. "Signiel," she said, and Millie nodded. "We have to talk," Dana added, her words weighty, but Millie simply nodded a second time and left the room. As she did, Dana could feel the butterflies in her belly and she desperately hoped her gut instinct was the right one.

What she didn't notice was the arrival of someone else – her guard friend from the front door. In fact, she didn't notice until she realised Boom was looking at him in some relief and when Dana turned the guard gave her the same sardonic look as before.

"Can I have my gun back?" he asked, politely, but without a smile. Dana looked at Boom and the guard and then turned and handed it over.

"Sure," she said with the sweetest smile she could muster, and to her surprise the guard smiled back.

"You are one crazy bitch," the guard said as he gave the gun a quick look over. "I've never been assaulted and had my gun stolen before. I might be in love."

"Oh, I try," she said, still uncertain as to the guard's intentions. Boom had started to get up, but the guard trained the Colt on him.

"I'm Jihoon," he smiled, before turning to Boom. "Don't move *byung shin*. There are some gentlemen out there who are not happy with you. You've drawn undue attention to our little operation."

"I don't understand," Dana asked.

"Gambling is illegal in Korea. For nationals, anyway. These little joints are pop ups but we can't afford to have the police looking into them. So, no unnecessary attention. And certainly no *bin dae sae ggi*."

"They stole my credit," Boom protested.

"Oh please, you stole from us," Dana pouted. "And you tried to kill me. *And you tried to kill me!* What the hell was that about?" Boom looked at her and Jihoon.

"Someone has a little problem. And not enough money to cover the problem," Jihoon said, supplying the answer.

"I got a call. Said if I dealt with you permanently all my money problems would go away. And I don't have a problem dealing with some talentless Australian," sneered Boom.

"Who?"

"These people don't give names," Boom replied, and Dana felt her stomach lurch.

"You're lucky I don't have the gun anymore," Dana growled. "What are you going to do with him?" she asked Jihoon.

"Oh, we won't kill him. That will make things more complicated. But I don't think Boom's little boy band is going to be a complete unit for the next few months." The look of panic on Boom's face gave Dana a small glow of satisfaction, and she turned to the door.

"Hey," Jihoon called to her. "Can I get your number?"

Dana paused for a moment, and then turned back with a smile. "Got a pen?" she asked sweetly. Jihoon tapped his pockets with his free hand.

"No," he said, disappointment etched all over his face.

"So close," she grinned, and gave him a kiss on the cheek. "Maybe next time?"

And with that she stepped out of the room. Jihoon turned back to Boom.

"Maybe I really am in love, huh?" he said with a smile. The gun now trained on Boom didn't look quite so happy.

XIII

Boom was hauled out of the building, looking far more miserable than Dana would have thought someone could look, though in all honesty, given the delicate and expensive jewellery he had stolen, and the fact he had tried to murder her, she found she didn't have a lot of sympathy for him. She suspected he was going to get quite the beating, but the truth was, Boom was a money maker, and presumably a useful asset, so he would be going on an unexpected hiatus for a few months before he returned to business.

"Hey," she said, and Jihoon turned, gripping Boom. "Maybe you didn't get a name, but who were they working for?" There was a pause, and Jihoon shook Boom.

"Answer the *yeoja*," he said. Boom seemed uncertain, and then opened his mouth. To Dana's astonishment, a neat little hole suddenly opened up in Boom's head, before a second opened on the opposite side, and blood started to dribble down his face. Boom's stressed look relaxed as he lost control of his muscles and then Jihoon dropped him, bringing his gun up to point at Dana.

But Dana was already looking for where the shot had actually come from. She saw movement from across the road, but as she took a step forward, her peripheral vision caught something to her right – a small figure in a suit, with white-blonde hair.

Dana dashed after the figure, but to her surprise, the person didn't run or hide. They simply turned and waited for Dana to catch up to them. This made Dana slightly wary, and she slowed as she approached the person, stopping so she didn't get too close.

She recognised the person immediately, remembering them from the Skybridge incident, the concert, maybe even when she had arrived earlier. Whenever she had seen the person before, she had felt uneasy, the germ of an idea that her killer might be the suited figure growing in her subconscious. But she had been wrong; they had been targeting Boom the entire time.

Dana paused and wondered what to say.

The person opposite her was Korean, wearing a black suit, with a black shirt and black necktie. The white, blonde hair was short and framed a face that was impish and cute, with thin lips and eyeshadow that created a strong cat-eye effect around the hazel eyes.

Dana opened her mouth to say something, but to her surprise, the person raised a finger to their lips.

"It's better this way," they said, their voice neither high nor low, but accented all the same. Then they smiled and brought out a key fob, which they activated. The bleep shocked Dana, and she turned to see she had totally missed the Lamborghini parked right beside them. Sleek and black with two cut-outs in the bonnet revealing the red underneath, like two fangs below the windscreen, the sports car had blended into the night perfectly. Now it lit up as the fob beeped. The person smiled again, and Dana was struck by how beautiful it was. Then they got into the car, and the doors were pulled shut behind them.

"Holy shit," Dana heard from behind her, a low whistle accompanying the comment. "You know that's a Sesto Elemento? You know how much that costs?" Dana turned to Jihoon who had followed her, but shook her head. Dana wanted to know so much more, but quietly and without fanfare, the car slid out of its park and into the night. The answers would not be coming in a hurry, and a shiver ran through her as she wondered who had authorised the justice she had just witnessed. Was someone tired of being cheated, or was something else involved – something she had encountered before? Or, worse, had the government decided to settle the score?

The truth was, she reflected, there was always a bigger fish out there waiting.

XIV

When Dana Spectra pushed the door to her room open, she saw, sitting on the floor looking very much like the shell of a human being, Millie. The room was warm, though outside it was still dark and cloudy, and it looked very much as though snow was about to disrupt Seoul's new day.

Dana shrugged her Angel Chen off, pulled her phone out from her back pocket and placed it on the closest flat surface near her (a small table that was to the side of the door) and sat down beside Millie. The girl was clutching Dana's bag to her chest, and she looked very shaken. Given everything that had happened, Dana supposed that wasn't an entirely unrealistic reaction. With all that, however, there was still one very important question unanswered.

"What were you doing there?" Dana asked, trying to keep her tone as free from judgement as she could. Millie looked at her, her eyes wide, before replying. Dana remembered reading somewhere that eye enhancement surgery was very popular in South Korea, as wide eyes and pale skin were the traditional markers of beauty in the country. Every country has its idiosyncrasies, Dana supposed.

"I thought you might need some help," Millie replied. "I know you told me to stay put, but I was worried about you. I didn't want anything to happen to you."

"How did you even know where to go?" Dana rejoined, and this time the doubt was clear in her voice.

"I didn't," the singer replied. "I just got in the back of the SUV and watched where you went after you got out. I have a key."

"Oh," Dana said, her voice small. The person she thought following her in the display building wasn't the guard at all. And the bump in the car hadn't been a bump at all, it had been Millie getting in the car, which was why the reverse sensors hadn't beeped. "That makes so much sense," Dana added. "You can sure get changed quickly."

"It's part of the job, right? I followed you and found the gambling den but I lost you. Then I found Boom and told him I wanted the jewellery."

"He took you inside to pretend to get it...he could have killed you, Millie!" Dana blurted out.

"I thought he'd just give the stuff up when he was caught. And there were so many people around they might have decided to kill some foreign girl. It's not like you're a crazy action girl spy or something."

"No," agreed Dana, crossing her fingers behind her back.

"Although the way you handled that gun," Millie added. "I mean, you were incredible."

"You can thank my dad," grinned Dana. "He was very keen I should be a good marksman." Dana reached forward and took the bag from Millie, not entirely surprised to feel her shaking. "You're an idiot," she whispered, and gave her a gentle push.

"What now?" Millie wondered. Indeed, Dana thought. What now?

Boom's death would come out, but Dana suspected it would be conveniently recontextualised, and Soojin...well, she would get over him. G'Star would be shaken, but the truth was they were part of a system, and there wouldn't be a lot of time to grieve. Rehearsal, promotions, recording, performing and advertising would ensure there would be virtually no time for Soojin to mope about the loss of her lover. Or the betrayal, which was probably more important in the long run.

But then there was Karim's problem of the agitator within Moonlight Entertainment. Having discovered Boom had stolen the jewellery and tried to kill her on the Skybridge, Dana had been convinced that she had found who Karim was looking for. The fact he wasn't Korean added to that cause as well. Except on the drive back, a clearer mind pointed out that he never admitted, or even suggested that he had killed anyone else. But he had been paid by…well, whoever he was about to reveal, so he probably could be easily bought. If Millie had killed those others…well, then she was an extraordinary actress. A simple night where a gun had been pointed at her head reduced the girl to a bundle of nerves (*was that really the definition of a simple night now?*). If she had killed people before, then the easiest way to find out if she was the killer would be to check her work-related activities the following day and see what state she was in, most of which could be found on YouTube. That's assuming she had time to pop out for a quick assassination between trips to the local convenience store. Truthfully, she had really got Karim his answer.

Ultimately ASIS' concerns seemed to stem from CIA worries, and the vague possibility that a North Korean was part of a K-Pop group that was becoming more and more successful. Maybe, just maybe, the earlier deaths were nothing but unfortunate accidents. It wasn't Karim's problem, it wasn't ASIO's problem, it wasn't ASIS' problem and it certainly wasn't her problem. And now, thanks to the well-dressed assassin, it wasn't even the CIA's problem.

"Fuck it," Dana decided. "I've got four more days here. Tell me I'm not going to be spending them alone," she added. She could still feel Millie shivering, and that alone convinced her she was making the right decision. If the CIA was right and someone was trying to shake confidence in the K-Pop industry, she wasn't a superhero. She reached out and grabbed the older girl's hand, feeling Millie squeeze back appreciatively.

The two stared out of the hotel windows and Millie rested her head on Dana's shoulder, as they watched the moonlight reflect on the Han.

THE END OF

THE KILLING LABEL

DANA SPECTRA WILL RETURN IN

SILHOUETTE